~ Look for these titles from Zoey Thames ~

CURVES FOR WOLVES

Quick & Sexy Wolves Book Five

Zoey Thames

etopia
press

Etopia Press
1643 Warwick Ave., #124
Warwick, RI 02889
http://www.etopia-press.net

CURVES FOR WOLVES

First Etopia Press electronic publication: November 2018

First Etopia Press print publication: January 2019

~ DEDICATION ~

To V.M. with love. And a special heartfelt thank you to everyone who has ever taken a chance on one of my books!

CHAPTER ONE

Cindy

After three years working as a limo driver for Mirage Confidential Limo Service, Cindy Taylor knew there were three things she really hated. Rush hour traffic. Red light cameras. And snowstorms.

Especially snowstorms.

Then again, what Texas girl in her right mind would actually *like* driving in the snow? She was far from San Antonio. Out here in Colorado, she saw far too much cold white powder falling from the sky.

Her hands gripped the steering wheel even tighter

as she eased the luxury limousine along the narrow road. She kept leaning forward to glance out the windshield past the tall slopes of the Rocky Mountains. It was dark out. The sky held that ominous look of low, gray snowstorm clouds.

Had she gone insane when she'd decided to leave Texas and move to Colorado? True, she loved the mountains, and yes, she'd desperately needed the work. But it was so cold here sometimes. And driving in the snow made her a nervous wreck and transformed her into a tightly wound ball of tension.

So far, her luck was holding. Not a flake had fallen tonight—yet. Maybe the good luck charm necklace she was wearing actually worked. She'd made the necklace of sterling silver, the graceful pendant holding a beautiful malachite stone of green swirls. The stone was supposed to bring luck in love too, but right now she'd settle for any luck that would help her avoid the storm.

She was driving the lower slopes of the Rockies. Even though there had been snowfall a day or so ago, the narrow, two-lane road was plowed, and ice wasn't a big problem. This should've been an easy assignment. But then bad weather had seemed to appear out of nowhere.

Right now, she was racing that snowstorm, trying to pick up a wealthy client and get him back to Boulder before the blizzard hit. Her satellite radio was tuned to a weather station. The cheerful weather reporter kept explaining how this surprise storm was going to be big—eight to ten inches of snow at least—and people should hunker down and stay off the roads if they could. She didn't have much of a choice. Driving millionaires and billionaires around Colorado was her job. Boulder, Denver, Castle Pines, sometimes even Aspen. Mirage sent her all over.

Ahead of her, the narrow road unrolled in a dark, winding path of asphalt. Tall evergreen trees flanked either side of the road, along with a barrier of old snow pushed aside by the plows. The night sky was covered by thick gray snowstorm clouds.

Her dispatch radio suddenly hissed and came to life with Amanda's cheery voice. "Cindy, this is Amanda back at HQ, do you copy?"

Cindy didn't take her eyes off the road as she eased the big vehicle around a sharp curve. The sign said to take the turn at twenty-five miles an hour tops. In these conditions, she took it at fifteen. Aside from the rare truck heading in the opposite direction, she hadn't seen much traffic at all.

She picked up the radio receiver when it was safe to do so. Amanda always referred to Mirage Confidential as "HQ," as if they were some kind of military force of limo drivers. It always made her smile. "I copy you, Amanda. But I'm a little busy."

"I hear ya. Right now you must be feeling like a two-tailed cat in a room full of rocking chairs."

More like a grumpy bear in a closet full of bear traps. Why had she agreed to this assignment again? Oh yeah. The thousand-dollar bonus. She could *really* use that money. So here she was, risking her life and her sanity on a winding mountain road at night with a blizzard on the way.

Crazy.

Or maybe she wasn't crazy, just dumb as rocks.

She couldn't say all of that over the open channel to Amanda at HQ. Instead, she said, "You got that right, Amanda. What do you need? The client didn't cancel, did he?"

If the client had canceled hiring the limo, she was going to go find him anyway and give him a tongue lashing he'd never forget in a hundred thousand years. Her tongue would be like a whip of outraged justice. So what if the guy was a billionaire a couple of times over? She would teach him some manners!

Or not. Because she really couldn't lose this job. Upbraiding the elite and executive clients of Mirage

Confidential was one way to quickly end up on the unemployment line.

"No, he didn't cancel," Amanda replied. "I'd pin his ears back if he did. I wanted to check in on you again. Radar shows that storm is right on top of you." The worry in her voice was clear even over the static coming from the radio speaker. "You sure you don't want to come back to HQ? All our other drivers are in."

She did want to head back, but according to the GPS, she was only two miles from the pick-up spot. "This guy's still paying that thousand-dollar bonus, right?"

"You know it, kiddo. It's specifically in the contract. You have the limo waiting on the road at the base of the mountain trail at eight-thirty, ready to pick up the client, and you get the bonus."

Cindy glanced at the digital clock. It was only fifteen minutes after eight. She was going to be early.

"You be careful, Cin. That blizzard's going to hit wicked hard. You make sure you pick this guy up and you drive right behind one of those plows all the way back to Boulder, you hear me?"

"I hear you loud and clear," she said, touched by Amanda's concern. Touched...and a little frightened. Colorado snowstorms were no joke. "Keep the lights on for me. I'll be back in the city in a hot minute."

Please, God, let me make it back to the city in one piece. Preferably before dawn, but right now, I don't mind it taking forever. I just don't want to freeze to death in the snow.

Her radio only spit out a burst of static. The storm must be interfering with the signal.

She frowned, an uneasy chill tickling up her spine. Without the radio, she suddenly felt very alone out here. She began to suspect that it had been a huge mistake to agree to pick up this crazy billionaire who, according to Amanda, had taken a helicopter to some high rocky slope in some extreme sport challenge to ski his way down to the bottom of the trail.

She snorted. Only someone with too much money and not enough sense would come up with something like that. Reckless, expensive, and stupid.

The client's name was Dalton Kincaid, a billionaire werewolf, exactly the kind of client Mirage Confidential specialized in. The fact that the client was not only a werewolf but a *male* werewolf explained it all. Human men were bad enough when it came to showing off, beating their chests, and doing needlessly macho (but sometimes sexy) things, but werewolves were even worse. She should know. She drove shifters around for a living. They were usually nice, perfect gentlemen, but they were always *intense*.

Part of Mirage Confidential's protocol was memorizing the client's file and information. Dalton Kincaid was thirty-two years old. Net worth of one point four billion dollars. He owned a diverse range of companies, funded hundreds of charities, had houses all over the world, a private jet and luxury yachts. He was an alpha wolf—leader of the Granite Hill Pack in Boulder. To top it all off, he was some kind of extreme sports guy, doing things like spelunking and freestyle skiing down virgin mountain slopes after jumping from helicopters. Insanity like that.

The dark road kept climbing steadily upward. She concentrated on it again. There hadn't been any traffic in either direction for the last few minutes at least. Her knuckles hurt from gripping the wheel too tightly.

Her heart sank when the first snowflakes began to fall. Several of them splatted against the windshield.

Great. The snowstorm had hit. Gritting her teeth, she pushed down on the pedal a little more, gaining a bit of speed before the snow got too bad.

But soon she had to slow way down again because the wind began howling down the slopes. Snow swirled and blew in all directions. She could barely see. She kept glancing at the clock, listening to the weather reports as she crept along the narrow road. The snow tires weren't gripping as well anymore. The limo was heavy, and that was good. But it wasn't very nimble, and that was bad.

She really started to sweat when the snow began to fall faster. It wasn't long before the snowfall was so dense it was like a white blanket. The wind began to pick up even more, rocking and shoving at the side of the limo facing the slopes.

But she was so close now that she didn't want to stop. She could still pick the client up on time. Then she could start back down out of the mountains. If she was really lucky, maybe the storm would be moving on by then.

Who was she kidding? As if she'd ever been lucky in her life. Wasn't that why she'd made her necklace in the first place? As beautiful as it was, it looked like the darn thing didn't work. And since she'd crafted it herself, she couldn't exactly take it to the store for a refund.

She was less than a quarter mile away from the pick-up spot when a gust of wind slammed into the broad side of the limo as she came around a curve. The tires slid on the snowy road. The back end lost traction and began to slide. Cindy sucked in a sharp breath as fear shot through her. Her heart began to pound hammer. She turned the wheel into the slide in order to keep control.

It should've worked perfectly. But on the curve, she ran out of road. She flinched as the limo slammed into the snow-covered guardrail. The guardrail buckled with a sickening crunch of metal.

Snow flew everywhere, blocking her vision even though the wipers were going as hard as they could. She cried out as the limo lurched and the front end went over the side of the slope.

The car slid down the slope as she stomped on the brake and turned the wheel, avoiding a tree trunk that whipped past her, taking off her side mirror. The brakes didn't slow the car much on the steep, snowy slope. She was gasping for breath, shaking from adrenaline as the car went careening toward the line of trees sixty or so feet down from the road.

"Shit!" she yelled, standing on the brakes as the heavy limo finally crashed into a tree with another heavy crunch.

The airbag deployed, and her seatbelt kept her safe. Cindy sat there in the driver's seat after the crash, trying to get her breathing back under control. Her hands were shaking. She stared out the windshield at the crumpled front end smashed into an innocent evergreen tree.

She had just crashed the limo.

She was not going to get that thousand-dollar bonus.

Laughing shakily, she closed her eyes. What was wrong with her? Had she hit her head or something? She had gone off the road in a *blizzard*. She had no idea when the next plow would come by. The driver wouldn't be able to see her from up there on the road. Not in a storm like this.

She was probably going to die out here. She'd be a popsicle. A Cindy-sicle. That wasn't even funny. How could her luck get any worse? She touched her necklace, suddenly wanting to roll down the window and chuck it out into the snow.

Deep breaths. Deep breaths. Get a grip. No, she wasn't going to die. She didn't even have a bruise from the crash, thanks to the seatbelt and airbag. She would call someone to come get her. No need to panic.

The wind howled. The snow swirled all around her. But the damage to the limo didn't look too bad. She put the car in reverse and tried to back up the slope to the road again.

The tires spun. The limo didn't move.

It was worth a try anyway. Clearly, she was going to need a tow truck.

"Okay, Cindy," she said aloud, ignoring the

tremble in her voice. "You didn't die. You aren't going to freeze. You aren't even hurt. Maybe your luck isn't so bad after all." She sat there for a second, staring out the windshield at the tree she'd hit, lit up by her headlights. She took a deep breath. "But talking to yourself just sounds crazy."

She reached for the radio receiver. "Amanda? This is Cindy. I had an accident. I'm off the road, and I need help. Do you copy?"

Nothing. Only static.

Either the blizzard was still interfering with the radio, or the crash had damaged it or the antennae.

She felt panic begin to nibble at her again. She pushed it back. Even if the radio didn't work, she still had her smartphone. She would just call for help.

Cindy reached into her pocket and pulled out her phone. She swiped it on. The phone told her that she had no bars. She was in a no-service area.

She cursed. Several times. In several colorful ways that would've mortified her mama.

Okay. Not the end of the world. So what if her limo was being buried in snow? At least the engine was running. She had heat, and the wipers were working—

A wolf jumped onto the limo's hood.

She screamed and dropped her phone. Quickly,

she hit the power locks. The car locked with a reassuring *clunking* sound. Then she stared at the huge gray and brown wolf standing on the hood. It stared back at her with golden eyes as the windshield wipers thumped and the snow fell all around it.

The wolf was a beautiful creature. A beautiful, scary creature. Its eyes were huge, strikingly golden…and intelligent. The thick fur was a dark gray with gradients of brown. The wolf was huge too. Much bigger than the wolves she'd seen in the zoo.

"Go away!" she yelled at it. Then she hammered on the horn.

The wolf didn't even flinch. In fact, it sat down on its haunches, still staring at her as if she were an exotic tropical fish in a tank. She had the feeling the wolf was laughing at her. Or maybe not laughing but certainly amused by her yelling. It was practically grinning.

Wait… That couldn't be an ordinary wolf—not at that size and with eyes that intelligent. It had to be a werewolf. Was it her client? Dalton Kincaid? Had he somehow seen the wreck and come to rescue her? But why would he change into a wolf and scare her half to death? Was her life turning into some kind of horror movie?

Suddenly, a halo of light began to shine around

the wolf's body. Swirls of golden light circled the wolf, making her squint. Her heart hadn't stopped beating fast since the accident, but now she realized she was going to see a werewolf changing shape. For all the dozens of shifters she'd driven around the state, she'd never seen one change form in person.

The wolf's body shifted, stretching and changing. It was made a near silhouette by the bright light and energy driving the physical change. The whole thing was breathtaking...and when it was over, she was staring at a very naked man crouched on the limo's hood.

He stood up, steam coming off his skin. Now she was looking up at him through the window, her eyes wide, her mouth gaping open. From this angle, it was impossible not to see his rather large, rather beautifully shaped cock. It was *right there*. Bold as day. It wasn't erect, but she could just imagine how big it would be if it had been—

Heat flooded her face even as a powerful surge of lust shot through her body, straight to her pussy. She glanced away, knowing she was blushing. Thank God she had locked the door, because there was a naked man on her hood. She glanced back at him, her gaze landing on his equipment again. He wasn't one of those men who manscaped either, and there was no reason why that should seem all manly and primal and turn her on. No reason at all.

She managed to tear her gaze away and look at the rest of the man. He was tall, dark-haired, wrapped in muscle and scars. And when she said *wrapped in muscle*, she meant it. He had washboard abs. He had tight, muscular pecs that she knew would feel hard as a brick wall. Broad shoulders. Thick biceps. Oh so many yummy muscles that made her nearly melt.

He was ruggedly handsome with a sharp jawline, dark with stubble, and piercing, light-colored eyes. Actually, he looked like he should star in some kind of western movie, either as the hero cowboy or the hard-edged villain. The intensity in his eyes belied the slight smile on his face.

She blinked. A strange werewolf was naked on her limo, and he didn't seem the least bit shy—or cold—about it.

"Are you hurt?" he asked, his voice deep but loud enough to hear over the wind, wipers, and through the glass.

"No!" she yelled back. "Now go away! And get off my hood! You're naked!"

She knew that didn't exactly make the most sense. If he went away, by definition, he would be off her hood.

But she was a little rattled right now. She'd nearly died driving off a mountain and hitting a tree, and then a wolf had turned into a naked man with a large penis right in front of her.

She shouldn't be thinking about that cock—no, she meant penis; "cock" sounded dirtier and even more distracting—so much, but what did you do when a man was naked *right there*? Maybe she should turn off the windshield wipers and let the snow block her vision of him.

And in a few moments, she definitely would do that.

The naked werewolf didn't get off her hood.

"Open the door," the man ordered. "I'll take you somewhere warm until this storm blows over."

His tone brooked no argument. It was as if he simply expected to be obeyed. Her hand had even moved toward the button to unlock the doors before she realized it. Which only made her angry.

"Are you insane?" she shouted. "I don't know you. You could be a crazy naked serial killer!"

She saw his smirk. It was impossible to miss. The arrogant bastard! Her hands bunched into fists as she glared at him.

The man pointed off into the trees. The expression

on his rugged face grew serious. "I live just over there. I came to help as soon as I heard the crash. Look, it's warm in my cabin. I promise you'll be safe. Another snowplow won't be along for hours. By then, this car will be buried."

"I'll take my chances with freezing to death!"

She thought she heard him growl with frustration and grumble something about stubborn females. What a jerk. Why was she not surprised?

"Ma'am, do you have emergency supplies in there?" the man asked. He finally hopped off the hood. The limo rocked on its springs. When he'd hopped off the hood, she'd been treated to a nice view of his ass. And she'd ended up biting her bottom lip to keep in a groan of pure lust. It wasn't fair for a crazy guy to look that hot.

He moved to the driver-side door. "Ma'am, can you hear me?"

She hesitated, watching him move. What kind of nudist serial killer called people "ma'am?" And wasn't he freezing his ass off? He probably had frostbite by now because he was barefoot in the snow…and maybe he could find a scarf or something to wrap around that cock. So maybe he wasn't a serial killer, but he sure was crazy.

She didn't answer any of his questions, even

though she knew there was an emergency kit in the trunk with flares, a first aid kit, and emergency blankets. She didn't want to tell him any more than she had to. Maybe if she ignored him, he would finally lose interest and go away.

Instead of going away, he bent down at the window, looking in at her. Snow was in his hair and melting on his shoulders. He frowned at her. "Open the trunk, and I'll check for you."

"No, thanks!" she said breezily, hoping he would get the hint and leave. Or at least put some clothes on so he wasn't so distracting.

"Open the trunk, ma'am," the man said, sounding as if he was working to keep his patience.

"No, thank you," Cindy repeated, giving him a sweet smile and tipping her jaunty chauffeur cap at him. "I'll just wait for help from the authorities. Thanks for all the concern, but you should probably be on your way. And maybe put some clothes on before you get frostbite on your favorite body part."

He grunted like some kind of caveman. She was used to rich, suave, and charming alpha werewolves. This guy was far rougher. Although none of those clients had ever called her "ma'am" either.

The man began walking toward the limo's trunk,

moving up the slope. She didn't adjust the side mirror so she could see his bare butt. She adjusted it because she needed to keep an eye on him for safety reasons. The butt view was just an unexpected perk.

He moved around the back of the limo out of view. Then she flinched when a rending, metal-tearing sound filled the air.

She turned in her seat, peering back through the limo's back window. Her mouth dropped open. The crazy werewolf had ripped the trunk lid completely off the limo. As she watched, he turned and flung the big piece of black metal off into the trees.

Cindy rolled down the window enough to stick her head out and yell. "You're going to pay for that!"

He didn't even look at her as he dug around in the trunk. "Send me the bill."

He pulled out the emergency kit from the trunk and shook out the shiny silver thermal blanket. He cocked his head and looked at it, then shrugged. He glanced at her and began to walk toward her through the swirling snow and wind again.

She ducked her head back inside the limo and pushed the button to raise the window again. He bent down at the window once more, looking at her with an eyebrow raised. Slowly, as if to avoid spooking her, he knocked on the glass and held up the thermal blanket.

"Here," he said. "Wrap yourself in this and come with me to my house. At least until the storm's over. Then I'll take you back to town."

She ignored him, still hoping he'd go away. She put both hands on the steering wheel and stared straight ahead at the tree she'd hit. She was praying he got the message.

"Ma'am," he said through gritted teeth. "I know you can hear me. You don't need to be afraid. I won't let anything happen to you."

Instead of answering, she picked up her cell phone and pretended to dial. Then she pretended to be having a conversation with someone on the other end, hoping he would finally get the hint and leave her alone.

This time, the shifter sounded as if he was struggling to hold back his amusement. "Ma'am," he said wryly. "There's no cell phone service here. Never has been, storm or no. So I'm not sure who you're talkin' to, but tell them hello from me. Oh, and maybe they can convince you to stop being as stubborn as an unbroken colt and come along with me somewhere safe and warm."

Her cheeks flared with heat. She knew they had to be bright red with embarrassment. She'd made a righteous fool of herself with the phone stunt, that was for sure. But Hell would freeze over before she admitted it to him. So she made a point of finishing her side of the imaginary conversation and then put the cell phone back in her pocket. She began to hum the theme song to the Jeopardy game show—oddly, the first thing that popped into her mind—trying to send him a message that she was still ignoring him.

Except, he wasn't giving up.

Except, he seemed to be the most stubborn, pig-headed male this side of the Rockies.

Instead of leaving, he grabbed the door handle and *ripped* the driver-side door off the hinges. She cried out in surprise as icy wind hit her and snowflakes blew into her face.

He held out his hand to her. She stared up at him with wide eyes, her heart pounding fast. She was terrified.

He seemed to realize how much he was scaring her and his eyes softened. "I'm not going to hurt you. You have my solemn word."

"You're not going to hurt me, but you're tearing my limo apart with your bare hands. That's not very reassuring!"

Again his lips quirked in a half smile. "Hate to tell

you this, sweetheart, but your car was destroyed before I got here."

"Don't call me sweetheart," she snapped. "And I was perfectly fine. The engine's still running, and I had heat. Then you *ripped* off the door, you pig-brained hooligan!"

He stared at her. She glared back at him, ignoring the swirling mix of emotions inside her. She was exhausted from all the fear and adrenaline since the crash. She was alarmed by how easily this werewolf had torn apart her limo—and now there was literally nothing between her and him. Locking the doors had been laughable. Mixed with that was the worry that her client was somewhere out in this blizzard, waiting for her to pick him up.

"Now that you mentioned it, I *did* open the door with a bit of force," he drawled. "No use crying over spilled milk. So now, why don't you kindly unbuckle and come with me? I'll get you somewhere safe and warm and get some food in you."

That sounded good, but she wasn't some stupid woman from a horror movie. You didn't go waltzing off into the forest at night with a strange, naked man.

"That's okay," she said. "I'll just sit here with the heater going until I run out of gas and freeze to death because some idiot werewolf nudist decided he couldn't open doors like a normal person. Don't mind me, thanks! Have a great day! Bye-bye!"

He stared at her.

Cindy gave him her best evil eye of death in return.

She was taking refuge in her anger. That was better than being afraid or breaking down in tears after the accident and losing her chance at that thousand-dollar bonus she really could've used.

Without a word, he reached across her and popped open her seatbelt. Then, easy as you please, he slid one arm beneath her legs, slid another around her waist, and lifted her out of the limo.

She squawked in outrage at being lifted out of the car. But she couldn't exactly hit him effectively from this angle.

She didn't have a chance to even scream or curse him. The man immediately turned and carefully set her down on her feet next to him in the snow.

"Now put that blanket on, ma'am," he said, pointing at the thermal blanket lying on the snow. "And come with me. We don't have far to go."

She spun toward him, drew her foot back, and tried to kick him in the balls as hard as she could. How dare he manhandle her like that? Why wouldn't this thick-skulled moron *listen* to what she wanted? She wasn't going to go anywhere in a blizzard with a naked werewolf stranger.

He effortlessly stepped out of the way of her kick. Almost as if he'd expected it.

She stumbled forward, off balance and flailing after missing. Before she could wheel on him and try punches this time—because obviously he would not listen when she used normal human words—he snatched up the blanket. Then with one amazingly fast and smooth motion, he wrapped her tightly in the blanket.

He wrapped her so tightly that she had her arms pinned. She felt like a swaddled baby. This was even more outrageous than the werewolf ripping apart her limo.

Before she could curse him, he swept her up in his strong arms again and pulled her tight against her chest. He carried her easily, and she was no skinny, delicate little thing. She had some meat on her hips and her bust and other places, but her weight didn't faze him in the least.

Wrapped tightly from shoulders to knees in a thermal blanket, she had no way to hit him. She could try biting him, but she was afraid that would only encourage him. He was a werewolf after all.

And clearly, he was a madman.

He looked down into her face with those piercing eyes that seemed both intense…and strangely kind. They were filled with concern.

No, that concern was probably because she'd nearly kicked him in the balls.

"I'm going to have to insist, ma'am," he said slowly. His mouth curled into a smile.

She hated that smile because it made her heart beat faster. Something else making her heart beat faster: being held against his firm, muscley chest. Which was just as hard and tight as it had looked.

"Let me go, you mangy hooligan!"

He snorted and ignored her demand. "My name is Cole Marsten. It's a pleasure to meet you."

"Well, it's not a pleasure to meet you!" she spat back at him.

"I'm sorry to hear that," he replied, not sounding sorry at all. He began to trudge through the snow with her cradled in his arms, the wind blowing his hair and snowflakes melting on his bare skin.

"You're kidnapping me!" she yelled.

"I'm helping you, woman," he said, his tone half growl, half exasperation.

"You're helping me against my will, you furry bastard!"

"I'm sorry, ma'am. But I won't leave a woman out here alone in a blizzard. It goes against everything I am."

She felt like her head was going to explode. "I wouldn't be in the snow if you hadn't ripped open my car like a can of tuna!"

He nodded as if that sounded about right. "I'll be happy to cook something hot and good to make it up to you. But first—and I feel like I've said this several times already—let's get you somewhere safe and warm."

She gaped at him, not knowing how to reply. He had kidnapped her from her car...and he wanted to cook for her?

Stupid, stubborn, bullheaded, brute of a man. That's what he was.

And yet...for all her outrage, she wasn't as afraid as she had been. Certainly she wasn't as afraid as she'd been when the limo had gone plunging down the slope.

There was something about him... Yes, he was sexy as hell. Yes, he was a dumb as a box of hammers, since he didn't seem to understand that she didn't want to leave her limo. But for all that, she didn't get the feeling that she was in danger.

She actually felt...safe.

It was surprisingly warm in this thermal blanket. Where his shoulder touched her, his skin felt hot. Wonderfully hot.

She pushed those thoughts away fast.

Pinned in this blanket and held in his strong arms, it looked as if she wasn't going anywhere except where he was taking her. For now at least. There was a blizzard raging around them, and even if she managed to escape, she would end up wandering through a snowstorm in only her chauffeur uniform.

Like it or not, it looked like she would be riding the storm out in his cabin.

But after the storm blew over, she was definitely going to press charges. If she didn't, who would ever believe all of this had happened to her?

CHAPTER TWO

Dalton

The wind moaned and buffeted Dalton from behind. Snow swirled all around him, making it hard to see more than thirty feet in any direction. His breath steamed out of his mouth, whipped away instantly by the wind.

It was dark. He was cold. His driver was late.

Dalton hated when people were late. It was a total pet peeve of his. He was never late, so he didn't think it was too much to ask that the people he paid actually do the same.

He tried to push down his ire, but it wasn't easy.

True, there was a snowstorm raging. True, he was asking a lot, having a chauffeur meet him in the lower slopes of the Rockies. But there was a reason he promised and paid huge bonuses to have the driver meet him at a very specific set of GPS coordinates at a set time.

Another big blast of wind howled down the Rocky Mountain peaks and slammed into his back. It was hard enough to almost stagger him. His wolf snarled at the wind, annoyed they were out in the storm. He kept his gloved hands in his ski jacket pockets and told his wolf to simmer down.

This morning, he'd been in Las Vegas. He'd taken a private jet to Denver, then hired a private helicopter to fly him and his skiing gear to Sugarloaf Mountain. The pilot dropped him off at the top of the peak. The helicopter skis touched the snow, but the rotors were still spinning as he climbed out. The helicopter flew off, leaving Dalton to face an adrenaline rush down otherwise inaccessible slopes. He loved the challenge, the pristine slopes, the thrill of going places most people couldn't reach.

Dalton wouldn't lie. He was an adrenaline junkie. His wolf loved a challenge. He was so damn rich, making millions was no longer a thrill, no longer a challenge. Nowadays, the only challenge he faced was how to give away the millions he was making year after year. No rival packs challenged his pack in Boulder or Denver. His wolf pack was happy and prosperous and at peace. He was single, but he played the field whenever he wanted. Women. Men. Both. He left either one satisfied if he did say so himself. Seducing women and men wasn't the same challenge these days.

So to keep his edge, he pushed himself by doing extreme sports. He drove his werewolf body to its limits. It was what kept him sharp. Strong. Fit. At the top of his game.

But now he was standing alone at the base of the Rockies, his skis and poles on one shoulder as he stared down the two-lane road that was rapidly disappearing beneath the snow flurries.

Where was this Mirage driver? The limo company's service was usually flawless, impeccable, which was why he used them. They specialized in catering to shifters and the like, promising the utmost discretion. And they always delivered.

Until now.

He glanced at the dark sky overhead, snowflakes spattering across his face. The storm was getting worse. His gear was the best money could buy, so he wasn't in danger of freezing to death. Werewolves ran hot anyway, and that meant he wasn't worried about frostbite. *Yet.* But he wasn't looking forward to hiking back to civilization in a snowstorm if his ride never showed. If anything, he'd ditch his skies and his clothes, shift, and run back to the nearest city as a wolf.

He pulled out his smartphone, yanked off one of his gloves, and swiped the screen. Snowflakes stuck to the display. He checked the time. His ride was now thirty-two minutes late. He hadn't received a call or text from Mirage, but then again, his phone was telling him he was getting zero bars and no service, so he couldn't exactly be annoyed by that. He'd been the one crazy enough to have a helicopter drop him off on a mountain so he could freestyle ski down virgin slopes, risking falls and avalanches.

Another flurry of snow swirled around him, icy cold, with the wind ripping at his clothes. The storm seemed to be getting worse with each passing moment. He prayed nothing had happened to the driver coming to get him. This storm wasn't supposed to hit yet, but it had surprised everyone with its speed and ferocity. He hoped the driver at least had chains on the limo. Otherwise, Dalton might be waiting here a while because they wouldn't be moving any time soon. These were treacherous driving conditions. In fact, he wasn't sure, but he thought he'd heard something off in the distance...something like the crunch of metal echoing off the slopes. But even though he had great hearing, the snowfall dampened sound.

Growling with frustration, he began to move around the edge of the lookout. He hadn't seen any traffic or snowplows in a long time. He walked around, holding his smartphone out, hoping against hope that he'd find a spot clear of the trees or the mountain slopes or a break in the storm and get some cell service.

He walked along the slope edge after climbing up the snow bank that had been pushed up over the guardrail by the snowplows. Still no cell service. He wasn't exactly shocked. He was miles and miles from—

The snow bank he was walking along while holding his phone up like a fool in the middle of a blizzard suddenly gave way. He scrambled for purchase, but the slope was steep, and the snow cover was breaking off around him in huge chunks, sending him tumbling down in a miniature avalanche.

The first thing he lost was his phone. It went flying out of his hands. The phone was lost in the tumble and the snow spray all around him and the snow coming down hard. He also lost his skis and ski poles.

He flipped himself onto his back, spreading his

arms and legs to slow himself and stop from rolling. Snow washed over him, getting in his face and eyes as he slid down the slope.

A tree trunk introduced itself to him. When he hit it, the impact knocked the breath from him. He slid down the slope another fifty or so feet before fetching up against another tree trunk. The small avalanche of snow half buried him.

It was very quiet as he lay there half submerged in the snow. Inside his head, his wolf was laughing at him, tongue lolling. The wolf was amused by strange things. Dalton cursed as he dragged himself out of the snow.

At least he was wearing waterproof clothing that resisted the wind, so he wasn't soaked to the bone. And speaking of bones, he hadn't broken any.

He dusted himself off and peered up the slope at the turnout. Half the slope's fallen snow had come down with him. He could climb it again, back up to the road. Or he could cut across the trees in a straight line to the lower road. Because right now, he pretty much knew his ride wasn't coming. So that meant he'd have to walk back to the nearest town. Or at least he'd have to walk until he could flag down a car or a snowplow or the storm finally blew over.

One thing he was certain of. He would never use

Mirage Confidential Limo Service again.

On second thought, maybe he was being too harsh.

Maybe he had his boxers in a twist having just fallen down a mountain slope.

No self-respecting werewolf feared a trek through a few trees. Or a forest. And a few snowflakes like this? This was nothing. As an alpha, he wouldn't turn aside from a challenge. Hadn't he grabbed about being an adrenaline junkie?

He set off trudging through the snow and the trees. The air smelled of snow and pine, even with the howling wind. He didn't bother looking for his phone. No one would be finding that thing until the snow melted, maybe in spring. It was worthless to him at the moment anyway.

For the first time, he began to think it might not have been the brightest idea in the world to jump out of a helicopter and ski down the mountain today of all days. It wasn't something he'd admit aloud to anyone else.

An alpha didn't admit mistakes. Not if he could help it.

He continued to forge his way through the snow, wishing he had his skis or snowshoes. Maybe he should shift into a wolf after all. He'd lose the clothes, but his fur would keep him warm. Also, he could travel faster. Walking through the blizzard was more challenging than he'd expected. It was easy to get turned around. He feared it would be easy to get lost. The wind interfered with his ability to scent and track, and the howling wind and the falling snow made it harder to hear.

He was about to stop trekking through the snow and shift to his wolf when he spotted the house. It was all lit up, every window on the bottom floor glowing, and he could see it even through the snow flurries. Smoke drifted from a big stone chimney, immediately whipped away by the fierce wind.

What the hell, he'd knock on the door and see if they had a landline that hadn't gone down in the storm. Or maybe they'd be friendly enough to let him ride out the worst of the storm by their fire. If they were good Samaritans, he'd be sure to make it worth their while as a thank you. After all, there were advantages to being worth billions.

The house seemed too big to be a cabin, but it was made out of logs, so he supposed it qualified. It was two stories, with a porch, green shutters, and a green door. The blinds were closed, but the windows still blazed with yellow light. Snow blanketed the roof, the wooden porch overhang, and buried the stairs.

He trudged through the snow toward the front door, moving past bushes and trees across the yard. He passed a wood chopping block and a huge mound of snow—a shelter for split wood. He stomped up the steps, shaking off the snow from his ski boots. Before he could raise his hand to knock on the door, the door swung inward, and a woman ran out.

Time seemed to slow when his gaze fell on her. It was like the kind of time slowing experienced during accidents or fights. But this came with another sensation. Or, more accurately, a few of them.

Dalton simultaneously felt like he'd been punched in the gut...and at the same time, that familiar lightning bolt of desire rocked him. Heat pooled down low as his groin tightened and his cock stiffened at the sight and scent of this woman. His wolf went wild, pacing in his mind, repeating something in his brain that had him reeling with shock.

"*Mate,*" his wolf practically howled in his mind. "*Our mate.*"

He barely had a chance to admire her long, auburn hair, her pretty, heart-shaped face, and her undeniable curves. He caught a glimpse of wide, pretty eyes before she was jumping down into the snow. The woman was wearing a uniform. Something that looked almost like a tuxedo, complete with a matching cap.

Wasn't that…a chauffeur uniform?

"Look out!" the woman yelled as she sprinted past him. "He's a crazy naked werewolf! Run!"

Dalton stared at her as she plunged through the snow without a jacket or boots. It was a wonder her cap stayed on without blowing away in the wind.

He didn't have a chance to say a word or react before a man wearing only boxer shorts burst through the door. He charged across the porch, chasing the human woman.

Dalton would've moved in the other guy's way to block him…except the exact same thing happened when he set eyes on the man as when he'd seen the woman. He felt like he'd been tackled, the breath knocked out of him. That same surge of desire had his cock all the way hard by now and straining against his ski pants. The scent of the other man was undeniably that of another wolf shifter. Time seemed to slow, and Dalton's wolf again went into a near frenzy.

"Mate," the wolf said, no hesitation in its mind.

The world had gone crazy. His wolf had gone mad. A woman chauffeur was running away from the tall, muscular man wearing nothing but plaid boxers in a blizzard. And Dalton's insane wolf was insisting that *both* of these people were his mates.

"Come back here, you damn-fool woman!" the man yelled as he charged past Dalton as if he wasn't even there. "Get back inside where it's warm, for the love of God! Please, woman. Show some sense!"

The man was a werewolf, a lone wolf by the scent, so he was fast. The little curvy human girl was never going to outrun him. Especially not in the snow.

Dalton had to do something. He had no idea what in God's name was going on here, but he was determined to get himself involved. A woman was running away from a man, so he didn't need to know the details to instinctively understand that she needed help.

And that meant kicking this guy's ass.

Dalton took off after him. The guy was fast, his muscles pumping and flexing as he ran. But Dalton was fast too. He managed to catch up and throw himself at the lone wolf. He tackled the other man, sending the two of them flying into the snow.

The other man bounded back to his feet almost instantaneously. A savage growl escaped his lips as the man faced off with Dalton, his golden eyes flashing and his teeth bared. Dalton jumped up again, fists clenched.

"We going to do this as men or as wolves?" Dalton snarled, cracking his knuckles as adrenaline rushed through him.

It had been a while since he'd dueled another wolf. No one had challenged him as alpha in years. He was looking forward to kicking some ass.

The man's intense stare narrowed even further. Then he seemed to dismiss Dalton entirely as if he wasn't worth the time or effort. Instead, he looked at the woman again.

The woman slid to a stop near the edge of the yard, a few steps from the evergreen trees. She had her arms wrapped tightly around herself as she shivered in the wind-driven snow.

"Don't go running off into this blizzard," the other wolf said, taking slow, measured steps toward her as if trying not to startle a deer. "Sit by the fire and get some food in you—"

Dalton wasn't going to let this bastard put his hands on her again. He lunged forward and swung at the other man, intending to lay him out.

The other werewolf dodged the punch effortlessly.

"You back-fighting son of a bitch," the man growled, low and angry.

Then he came at Dalton. They fought each other hand to hand. Dalton was used to fighting in wolf form, but he was still strong and fast in human form. The problem was, this guy seemed just as strong and fast.

They traded punches. Dalton landed a few good ones. Unfortunately, the other guy landed more than his share of good ones too. Both their wolves were in full fight mode, neither one of them willing to give an inch. Snow fell all around them. The icy wind pushed and bit at them. As they fought, they trampled snow and kicked up snow.

"Stop fighting!" the woman suddenly yelled, surprising them both. She didn't come between them, so she clearly wasn't a fool. But from where she stood shivering near the trees, it was obvious the savagery of their fight dismayed her. "*Stop* it!"

By some unspoken agreement, they both stopped fighting and looked at her.

Dalton knew it was strange. Once two male wolves went at it, they generally didn't stop until one of them yielded or couldn't fight on. But this human girl had stopped them both with four words.

His wolf had been lost in the frenzy of the fight, but now it grinned in his mind and told him calmly, "*She's our mate.*"

As if that explained why she could have such power over him. So why had this other wolf stopped as well? What the hell did *that* mean?

Dalton looked her in the eyes. She truly was stunning. Auburn hair beneath that cute little uniform hat. Vibrant, almost hypnotic green eyes staring at him from a pretty, heart-shaped face. Curves that made him have to bite back a groan. Her professional uniform only served to enhance those curves, even though the uniform wasn't designed to be anything but professional. Large breasts, wide hips, thick thighs that had his cock stirring to life again, despite all the adrenaline roaring through his veins.

God, why did he want to stop fighting right now and march over and claim those full lips of hers with his own? How did one human female have that much hold on him—and he didn't even know her name? From her chauffeur's uniform, he was sure she had to be the Mirage driver who was supposed to meet him at the base of the mountain. He had no idea why she was out here in the middle of nowhere.

But he was very interested to learn the answer.

"All right, sweetheart," the other wolf drawled. "We stopped fighting. Now, will you stop running off like a spooked colt and come back inside?"

"She's not going anywhere with you, asshole," Dalton growled. His fists clenched again. Who the hell was this guy?

The other wolf turned icy blue eyes to him. When their eyes met, Dalton felt his body tense and his heart begin to pound faster. For a second, it felt like he'd grabbed a live wire with his bare hands. His wolf snarled in his head, but he could sense the beast's conflict. Because at the same time, his wolf was attracted to the man.

"Don't fight our mate," his wolf chastised him.

If they hadn't been fighting over a woman, it would've been easy to understand why his wolf was so conflicted. The other man was tall, muscular, with broad shoulders wrapped in muscle, a set of six-pack abs that Dalton already knew felt hard as steel, since he'd punched those abs a couple times during their fight. His eyes had a predator intensity, a strength of will that Dalton's alpha side immediately recognized. The bastard was only wearing boxer shorts, probably because he'd shifted recently, so he had to be freezing his balls off out here, even though werewolves had higher internal body temps.

On top of all that, he was handsome, which pissed Dalton right off. Not just good-looking, but that rough-and-ready, turn-heads kind of handsome. Dalton was used to being one of the best-looking males in the room, but this guy gave him a run for the money.

It all made him want to punch the jerk right in the jaw.

The other shifter drew a hand across his mouth to wipe away the blood where Dalton's fist had caught him. His hand rasped against his dark stubble, the sound sending a raw and unwelcome thrill of desire racing through Dalton's body.

"Now just who the hell are you, buddy?" the man demanded in a deep, rough voice. "And why are you on my land, fighting me in a blizzard?"

Dalton rubbed his jaw where the guy's fist had clipped him a good one. "I'm Dalton Kincaid. And right now, I'm coming to the aid of a lady in need."

The man chuckled. A slow grin spread across his face as he glanced at the human woman again. "Lady in need? I don't see any lady in need around here. But I do see one stubborn hellcat too foolish to know what's good for her."

The hellcat in question put her hands on her hips and glowered at the man. "You bastard! Just because I don't want to be kidnapped and eaten by a crazy mountain-man werewolf, that makes me a fool?"

Dalton started toward her, holding his hands up to show her that he meant her no harm. "Did he hurt you, Miss?"

She hesitated, frowning. Her eyes cut back to the other wolf, lingering a bit long on the guy's body. The wind meant Dalton couldn't catch her scent, but he would've sworn her cheeks heated. "Well…no. He didn't hurt me."

The other wolf tipped an imaginary hat at the woman…which made Dalton want to fight him all over again. The jerk was really playing up the backwoods cowboy bit.

"I appreciate you speaking the truth, ma'am," he said. "I'd hate to have to keep kicking Mr. Kincaid's ass over this unfortunate misunderstanding."

Annoyance flashed through Dalton. *Whose ass was being kicked?* he almost demanded, but the human woman beat him to the punch.

"But you *did* kidnap me totally against my will."

That seemed to amuse him. "I reckon most kidnappings are against *one* person's will at least."

"Don't be an ass," Dalton warned, showing his teeth again. "Did you kidnap this woman?"

The guy crossed his arms over his broad, muscular chest. The icy wind blew through his hair and sent snowflakes swirling all around him. "She was in a wrecked car, determined to freeze to death out in this blizzard. So I brought her here."

"You wrapped me in a blanket and manhandled me!" the woman said, sounding highly annoyed.

Dalton paused. It sounded a little odd to hear someone wrapping the person they were kidnapping in a blanket and carrying them off. Maybe there was more here than he first realized.

He turned back to the other wolf. "You manhandled her?"

The guy shrugged. "There was as little manhandling as possible."

"Why was she running from you, then?" Dalton demanded. His hands balled into fists again. He was ready to get back into the fight if he heard the wrong answer.

The other shifter shrugged again. "I have no idea. I put her on the couch. Then I bent down to put a few logs on the fire. This wild woman jumped up, grabbed a piece of firewood from the pile, and clobbered me with it. Then she ran out into the storm like a mad woman."

He shook his head as if he still couldn't believe it.

Dalton laughed. He couldn't help it. He was too far from the woman to catch her scent because she was downwind of him, but he could catch the other shifter's scent easily enough. The guy wasn't angry or enraged. He was frustrated and annoyed…and a little amused. He even seemed to feel a grudging respect for the woman too. And desire…

That made Dalton's wolf side conflicted again…and the human side as well. Because he felt just as attracted to the woman as this other guy seemed to be. Unnervingly attracted to her. Sure, she was pretty, but the world was filled with beautiful women. Yet this one, on first sight, had caught his attention in a way no other female had for a very long time, if ever.

So if this other wolf was feeling the same, there might be another fight coming very soon.

He turned to the woman. Just looking at her sent another surge of desire crashing through him. He was as bad as a horny teenager around her. That realization unsettled him, but he pushed the thoughts aside for later. First, he had to find out what the hell was going on. He was the only one even remotely dressed for the weather, and he could see the human woman was already shivering badly.

"You work for Mirage Confidential?" he asked, going with his gut assumption.

She nodded. "You're Dalton Kincaid." A shy smile appeared on her face. It was utterly endearing and nearly won his heart. God, he was such a fool. Maybe he'd hit his head during the avalanche and it had turned him into a sucker for a pretty girl's smile. "I'm Cindy Taylor," she continued. "Your driver for the evening. If we still had a limo, that is. I'm afraid it went over the cliff."

Before he could take that in completely, the other shifter began to speak.

"There was an accident," the man said. "On my land, near one of the curves in the road. She went over the edge and smashed up against some trees. There's no way a tow truck can get here until the storm blows over." He looked from Dalton to Cindy and back again. "So, what do you say we stop acting like a bunch of mooncalf idiots and get inside where I have a fire? We can talk more when we're warm."

Dalton glanced at Cindy. "If the limo's wrecked, and the storm's still in full swing, I say we take him up on his offer. Some heat will do us all good. We'll wait out the storm and then get help." He held her gaze, looking deep into her big eyes. "I don't think either of us has any other option."

She still hesitated, clearly torn.

"I'm a pack alpha," he assured her. "I have a lot of experience reading other werewolves." He jerked a thumb in the other shifter's direction. "This guy might be crazy enough to live out here in the wilderness alone, but he doesn't want to hurt you. I can sense it. Call it alpha intuition." He grinned at her. "Besides, I'll be right here to protect you. You have my word."

The other wolf grunted but didn't say anything else. Clearly he wanted her inside and out of the storm as much as Dalton did. The other shifter was willing to let a backhanded challenge slide to get what he wanted.

Interesting.

Cindy finally nodded and began to walk toward them again. Dalton couldn't help it. His protective instincts would not be denied. He unzipped his heavy ski jacket, took it off, and held it out to her. "Put this on."

At first, he thought she might refuse. There was a spark in her eyes, a flash of annoyance as if she didn't like being ordered around. But she did take the jacket, and she did put it on. So she might be stubborn, but she wasn't a complete fool.

He walked on one side of her, trying to control the desire to wrap his arm around her and shield her from the wind with his body. He didn't want to spook her. She was a driver for Mirage, so she had plenty of experience with shifters, but still, out here in the wild, after an accident and with a storm raging, he didn't blame her one bit for being a little jumpy.

What he didn't like was how the other wolf took his place on the other side of her as if he was guarding her too. And even though she glanced at him, she didn't run. In fact, Dalton didn't scent any fear from her at all. She was actually feeling safer now. Protected.

Maybe seeing two werewolves battle it out for you in the middle of a blizzard did that for a woman. He shook his head. He would never understand humans. And as much as he loved them, he would never fully understand females either. Being bi meant that he at least understood the males in his life. Fighting. Fucking. Food. The three core "F's" of being male. He guessed this other wolf would agree.

"I didn't catch your name," Dalton said to the other werewolf as the three of them crossed the yard, trudging through the deepening snow back to the shifter's house.

"Cole Marsten," the other man said. He gave that charming, lopsided grin again. "I'd shake your hand, but since we've already punched each other in the face several times, I'd say introduction handshakes aren't necessary."

Dalton nodded, but he stuck his hand out anyway. "Maybe you're right, but it never hurts to be civilized."

Cole chuckled, glanced at his hand, and then shook it. They were both shaking hands in front of Cindy, so she had to stop and wait while they did so. She looked at each of them in turn.

"I'm glad everybody's getting along," she said wryly. "But can we get inside where it's warm? I know I have some extra padding, but I'm really freezing my ass off right now."

"Says the woman who ran out into a blizzard in the first place," Cole grumbled under his breath. Although he was still smirking.

"Now don't you start," Cindy shot back, glowering at him.

Dalton shook his head. This was going to be one hell of a night.

CHAPTER THREE

Cole

A damn mess, that's what this was. Cole should've stayed in his house when he'd heard the unmistakable sound of a car hitting the guardrail. But he'd had to be the hero. He'd shifted into his wolf and gone bounding off into the storm, eager to help.

He shook his head and snorted. As if he could ever turn his back on someone who needed help. That wasn't how he'd been raised. So mess or not, he was in it up to his neck now.

He'd found the limo crashed at the bottom of a

steep slope. He'd been relieved that the human woman inside wasn't hurt, but she'd turned out to be stubborn as a tired mule. Not that she looked anything like a mule. The gal was downright gorgeous. With pretty eyes that matched that striking piece of jewelry around her neck, and the way her uniform complemented all those wonderful curves. Full lips that looked soft, tempting, and warm.

Too bad she thought he was some kind of criminal. You'd think she'd never laid eyes on a naked werewolf before, the way she'd gawked at him. It might've been amusing, if she hadn't been so damn obstinate.

He hadn't meant to scare her. Or to put his paws all over her. "Manhandling" was what she'd called it. But he couldn't leave her out in the storm. Even if the limo's engine had been running and she'd had heat, he knew there was no cell reception out here. He also knew the limo would end up buried in snow before the blizzard blew over. So he'd taken matters into his own hands.

Maybe that had been a mistake.

Hell, it *had* been a mistake. Because the instant he'd opened the door—no, that wasn't right. The moment he'd *ripped* the door off its hinges and caught her scent, he'd nearly staggered from his reaction to her.

His wolf had gone wild. So had his body. It was as if he'd been hit by a tractor trailer.

Mate. She was his mate. There was no question about it. His wolf agreed. His own mind agreed. Everybody agreed.

Except her, of course.

So he'd kidnapped his mate—according to her anyway. He'd done it for her own good, but when he'd had her wrapped in the blanket, in his arms, pulled close against his body to give her heat, it had been pure hell to keep thinking of Solitaire and shoeing horses and doing the dishes—anything to keep his cock from going erect. He knew that would have freaked her out beyond recovery. So he'd used every ounce of willpower he possessed to keep the instant, powerful desire he felt for her under control.

He didn't need this. Not at all. There was a reason he lived out here in the mountains, way the hell away from humans or other shifters. People brought problems. Complications. It was inevitable. People were like cats infested with fleas. They might even be cute, but then you woke up with fleas of your own.

He stopped himself from shaking his head again as he put another log on the fire. He was shaking his head so often, they would think it some kind of nervous twitch.

His head still ached too. The last time he'd tossed a log on the flames, the woman had smacked him right on the head with a piece of firewood. She was some kind of spitfire, that was for damn certain.

He actually admired her for it. Too bad he'd just been trying to help. He thought she'd calm a little after he'd put on some boxers, but before he could get around to putting on proper pants, the whole fireplace episode had happened.

Then the chase had gone down. Then this other blasted alpha had shown up out of nowhere. Dalton Kincaid. The man reeked of money. It was everything from the high-end outdoor clothing he wore to his carefully manicured hands. Rich man's hands. Well, they did have some calluses, so the son of a bitch wasn't a complete milksop. And the bastard could fight.

Cole glanced over to where Dalton was sitting on the couch next to Cindy, both of them near the fire. She caught him looking.

"I'm glad you finally put some pants on, Mr. Marsten," Cindy said to him. He was surprised to see the slightest hint of a smile on those full lips of hers. "Most men would've been afraid of frostbite on certain sensitive areas, but not you."

Her sass amused him. "Most wolf shifters run hot." He allowed a cocky smile to cross his face. "Guess I run hotter than most."

Dalton chuckled. Cindy's cheeks only went a little pink, and her nostrils flared, although she said nothing else. He had no idea why that confounded woman hated him so much. The crazy thing was, she was the female his wolf was claiming as a mate. The girl who'd run away from him every chance she got. The one who had smacked him on the head with a log.

Wonderful.

He bent down at the fireplace and stirred the coals. The fire had nearly gone out with all the ruckus. He placed another couple of split logs on the coals. He was careful to place them so there was good air flow. Then he used the bellows to blow air on the coals, teasing back a flame.

Soon he had the fire roaring again. Heat radiated through the room. He loved the feeling of heat coming off a wood fire. It was somehow different from the warmth of electric heaters or even from a gas fireplace. He loved the sounds of a good fire too. The crackling and popping. But there was also no denying the beauty of a fire. The drifts of sparks. The orange-red glow of the coals. The dancing flames, moving like they were alive.

The scent of smoke and charcoal.

A real fire on a winter's day was one of his favorite things. Always had been. Always would be.

Well, for the man part of him, anyway. The wolf part wasn't too keen on flames. But his inner wolf always tolerated the humanlike parts of him it saw as strange. Just like the man part of him tolerated the yearning to howl and sing wolf song and track prey through the snow.

Of course, he wasn't sure that tolerance extended to claiming strangers as their mate.

Behind him, Cindy laughed softly, startling him out of his thoughts.

"I haven't been around a real fire since Girl Scout camp," she said. "I forgot how beautiful it is."

He glanced at her, smiling. He wasn't really a sharing kind of guy, but he surprised himself by proving that wrong. "It's one of my favorite things. A healthy fire in a fireplace on a cold night. I love the color and warmth of the light. And how the waves of heat wash against your face."

He shrugged, suddenly uncomfortable that he'd said so much.

"You're a poet," Dalton said, a little smirk on his face that Cole didn't really care for.

Cindy frowned at Dalton. "I think what he said was perfect and absolutely true. In fact, I couldn't agree more." She held out her hands toward the fire, clearly reveling in the heat.

Dalton seemed to be caught off guard by Cindy's defense of Cole. He wasn't the only one, because Cole was caught off guard by it as well. Especially since the little human had been determined to defy him all night long, no matter how much he wanted to help her.

Cole couldn't help a little smirk of his own at Dalton. He knew he shouldn't gloat because he had a sore spot on his skull from where Cindy had already whacked him with a fireplace log. So he shouldn't get too comfortable or start thinking she was ever going to be one of his biggest fans.

Dalton's expression darkened. He knew Cole was gloating...and he didn't like it.

Too bad, bucko, Cole thought, turning back to check the fire again. He bet a rich guy like Dalton really hated not to get his way. That made it all the sweeter.

"How long until the storm's over?" Cindy asked after a few minutes had passed.

"A few hours. Maybe a little more," he replied. "These storms in the mountains are no small deal."

Dalton grunted and leaned back on the couch

nearer to Cindy.

Cole didn't like the guy sitting so close to her. His wolf was already growling in his head, telling him he needed to defend his mate. But the wolf was also confused, and that wasn't normal. Because while the mate signals were undeniable from Cindy, he was also getting them from that rich bastard, Dalton.

And what the holy hell was *that* all about?

"At least you still have power," Dalton said. "You'd think a storm like this would knock—"

As if on cue, the lights flickered and went out. The living room was plunged into darkness broken only by the warm orange glow of the firelight.

Cindy drew in a sharp breath. Cole could scent her sudden burst of fear.

He reached out and took her hand in his. She had cold fingers, despite the fire, so he clasped them, wanting to warm them. He looked into her wide, vulnerable eyes.

"Give it a second," he murmured.

The lights blinked back on. Very faintly, he could hear his emergency generator rumbling away. With the generator, he had more than enough power to ride out the storm.

She laughed, touching her throat with her other hand. Gently, she pulled her hand from his. But was it his imagination, or had she squeezed his hand a little as she withdrew? He thought it might be a silent little "Thank you."

He would definitely accept that.

"You have a generator," Dalton stated. Cole could hear some grudging respect in his voice.

"Can't live out here without one. Or at least you'd be a fool to try. Like I said, these winter storms can be real fierce."

Dalton narrowed his eyes and edged the slightest bit closer to Cindy. "I'm surprised. I thought a lone wolf out here would be more the mountain-man type. Really roughing it. Like in the old days."

He grinned, ignoring the insult. For Cindy's sake. "I've got my own built-in fur coat, but it would be a real pain in the ass if my pipes all froze. Besides, a man can live away from civilization without being a damn fool."

"I'm not convinced of that yet," Dalton shot back.

Cindy put a restraining hand on his arm and Dalton subsided. Which was a strange bit of business, seeing as Dalton had been the one to hire her as a driver. He couldn't help but be curious about the whole arrangement. Seemed odd to hire someone else to drive you around like a king in a litter. Maybe that was because Cole actually enjoyed driving his truck. But to each their own, he supposed.

"So…" Cole said, turning his gaze back to Cindy. He stopped short because *damn*. She really was one fine woman. He didn't want to stare, but he couldn't help it.

She was pretty, yet that was an understatement. It was those damn eyes that seemed to punch right at his heart. They were so big and full of expression. This human woman didn't have a poker face. Not even close. Every emotion inside her was easy to see in her green eyes. He found himself liking that. It made him feel like he could trust her—or at least understand her. Dalton was different. He was much closer to what Cole was used to with other alpha wolves. But Cindy…she had a sweetness to her.

When she wasn't acting like a stubborn hellcat, that was.

And her scent. God above him, he swore it was driving him wild. He wanted her in his arms again. Now. He wanted to nuzzle her neck, breathing in her unique female scent, and then kiss his way up to nibble on her earlobe. Then he would claim those full lips of hers, kissing her until she was breathless and yielding. And then he would really make her feel good…

He suppressed a growl as he looked away from her gaze. Part of him was afraid she'd see his desire, his passion in his eyes, no matter how much he tried to hide it. Thank God he had pants on now. He didn't need his cock betraying him by standing up hard and erect, telling all the world how fucking turned-on he was. How much he wanted to plunge deep into her wet heat. How much he wanted to hear her breath come faster and faster as he drove her to the heights of bliss —

Dammit, he needed to stop. Right now.

He shifted positions, trying not to draw attention to the uncomfortable throbbing press of his cock against his pants. If she saw that monster and realized it was for her, she might just run right back out into the blizzard.

Either that or she'd try and hit him with a piece of firewood again.

To distract himself, he pressed on with the small talk. Hell, he was terrible with small talk, but he had to do *something*.

He cleared his throat and started over. "So you were supposed to pick him up?" he said to Cindy, then glanced at Dalton. "Before the crash?"

"That's right," she said. "I work for Mirage Confidential. We specialize in high-end clients. We're a luxury transportation service without equal."

He chuckled. "That sounds like it came right off the brochure, ma'am."

To his delight, she laughed too. "I know, right? They drill it into your head. I can spit it out like a robot." She hesitated. "But you can call me Cindy."

He nodded solemnly at her. "Pleased to meet you, Cindy. Sorry we got off to such a rocky start."

Her cheeks flushed. And damn if he didn't see a flash of heat in her eyes. He suspected she was thinking of him standing naked on the hood of her limo. Either that or she was remembering how it felt to be in his arms. He bit back a triumphant grin. His little stubborn mate might even be coming around.

"Sorry I hit you with a piece of wood," she said.

Dalton threw back his head and laughed. At first, Cole was annoyed. He might need to explain to this blue-blood Dalton bastard how unwise it was to laugh at a wolf like Cole. Explain with his fists anyway, teaching the guy another lesson. But then he willed his fur to stop bristling and he grinned instead. Because it *was* kind of funny. Not at the time. And the ache in his head didn't fully agree. But it did show the feisty human had some real fire.

He respected that.

"Forgiven," he said with a wave of his hand. "I realize I can be a bit bullheaded when I see something that needs to be done. My mama would've named me a fool for tossing my manners out the window, but I wanted you safe."

Now she truly was blushing. The color in her cheeks was softened some by the firelight. He felt his heart squeeze in his chest. Damn. Damn. *Damn*. He'd never had a woman—or a man—affect him so strongly. Hell, he was no stranger to lust and the heat of passion and the drive to fuck. Before he'd gone wandering away from civilization, he'd caught plenty of tail, female and male. But just watching her made his heart ache. It stirred powerful feelings inside him that he thought had gone forever.

Dalton interrupted the turmoil of his thoughts. "Maybe next time you can slow down a little and not act like such a caveman."

Cole turned his gaze to the other alpha. He wasn't smiling now. The guy definitely had a problem with Cole. Probably because Cole had been kicking his ass in their fight. Alpha wolves hated to lose. Rich, snobbified alphas hated it even more.

He gave a wolfish grin, pun intended. "Can't blame a man for losing his head over a pretty lady."

He was delighted to see Cindy's flush deepen and her pupils dilate. Dalton could give him shit all he wanted, but Cole was going to keep right on with what he was doing. Scoring points with Cindy. He wanted her calm and relaxed and feeling safe. Then, after he dug them out of the snow and drove her back to town, she'd be certain to want to see him again.

From there he could think of hundreds of delightful opportunities.

But first, he had to deal with the Dalton character. The bastard was too damn slick and good-looking for his own good. Cole didn't like how his wolf was drawn to the other man. It wasn't submission. It was attraction.

And that might be a problem.

He turned to Dalton, taking his time, enjoying the heat from the fire as it warmed his skin. "So why did you have a chauffeur come all the way out here to pick you up in a limo? You got skiing gear, but you don't have a truck?"

Any man who headed into these kinds of conditions without a truck was begging for trouble.

"Yeah, I own a truck," Dalton replied. "Among other vehicles. But it's not here because I came in a helicopter."

Cole raised an eyebrow. Of course. Helicopters. Why hadn't he thought of that?

"A little risky flying a helicopter in a blizzard," he said wryly.

Dalton sighed as if he were dealing with a real idiot. "I was flown in hours ago." He pointed to his ski boots. "I free ski down the slopes as a challenge." He shrugged and flashed a cocky-as-hell grin. "I don't do bunny slopes. These days, I don't even do ski resorts. Extreme skiing or nothing."

Cole hated to admit it, but that was pretty damn ballsy. He respected that, even if it did seem like a damn-fool thing to do, risking your ass in avalanches and plunging off cliffs just for some sports thrill.

"To each his own, I suppose," Cole drawled in reply.

He could see Dalton didn't like that, but the man kept silent. Cole realized it was time to start being a good host. Maybe he could be excused for punching Dalton around a little outside when werewolf blood had been hot and he'd been with—

"With our mate," his wolf interjected into his thoughts.

—with a lady in distress. But his mama would've tanned his hide if she'd seen him being rude and ungentlemanly to folks in need. Even if one of those folks had enough money to waste hiring helicopters.

He smiled at Cindy, then nodded at Dalton. "Y'all are welcome to ride out the storm here with me. I'd be honored to have you as guests."

"It's not like we have much choice," Dalton grumbled.

"Don't be like that," Cindy scolded him, frowning.

Her reprimand surprised both of them, but Dalton seemed far more surprised than Cole. It looked like Dalton wasn't used to being scolded by the people he hired. Cole tried to hide his grin and wasn't entirely successful.

Cindy's big eyes looked into Cole's. Damn, he could easily get lost in those eyes and never want to come out.

Listen to him. He sounded like a damn love-struck fool. It was downright embarrassing.

"Thank you for…for everything," Cindy said quietly. She hesitated, then she licked her lips. Seeing that sent a lightning bolt from his brain right down to his cock.

Dalton seemed to regain his footing after Cindy's rebuke. He slowly nodded to Cole. "I appreciate the hospitality." He also paused before pushing on. "Thank you."

Cole nodded back. He had to respect that the man had said thank you, despite the fact that he looked like he'd swallowed a lemon when he said the words.

He glanced at the cabin's front windows. The snow was still coming down fast. It tapped against the glass as the wind howled and drove it under the porch eaves and against the house. He searched his mind for a way to pass the time that wouldn't be awkward or tense.

Hell, food always brought people together. When in doubt, his mama always fed him and his brothers…and their friends and girlfriends. Hell, she even fed strangers in need from time to time. It was always a good time. Since he was a man who knew his way around a grill, it was time to find out if his guests were hungry.

"How do you feel about steak?" he asked. "I have a few marinating in the fridge. We could have some frozen French fries." He glanced at Cindy. "You aren't a vegetarian, are you? Because I could do some stir-fry too."

"I like steak," she said. "And French fries. Even stir-fry."

"*I'm* a vegetarian," Dalton growled.

Cole did a double-take. "You?"

What kind of werewolf was a vegetarian? He didn't think it was even physically possible.

A grin spread across Dalton's face. "All right, I made that up. Steak would be great."

"That's more like it," Cole said. Dalton's little joke had caught him off guard. Maybe the rich guy didn't have a telephone pole shoved up his ass after all.

He stood and stretched, loving how the heat that had built up in the fabric of his pants pressed against his legs. He was actually looking forward to getting something in his stomach. Food brought people together, right?

Wait. What the hell was wrong with him? He didn't want to bring Cindy and Dalton together. That would be a disaster.

He pushed those worries aside. Right now he had a mission. He had a job to do. He was going to feed these two—

"*Mates,*" the wolf insisted, thoroughly annoying him. "*Take care of our mates.*"

—these two *guests* of his. Then he'd set them up with somewhere to crash for the night. Tomorrow morning he'd plow the driveway leading to the main stretch of road, and he'd take them both back to town. From there, they could get a tow truck to retrieve the limo.

They would be out of his hair. He would be back to living alone. He wouldn't have two strangers crashing his territory. The human wasn't bad, but another alpha wolf? He didn't know why his wolf wasn't going for the other shifter's throat right now.

Besides, there was no way these two were really his mates. A human and an alpha shifter who both happened to show up during a blizzard? The chances on that were a million to one. Cole wasn't a betting man.

So what the hell did that mean?

Why was he suddenly uneasy, as if he didn't want to find out the answer? As if he was afraid these two might change his laid-back life forever…

He shoved those worries aside and strode toward the kitchen. When a man got to thinking too much, it was best to lose himself in some work. He had some cooking to do for his guests. That was enough.

For now.

CHAPTER FOUR

Cindy

It was so quiet here. Cindy leaned back on the couch. She felt surprisingly calm and at peace, especially since she'd gone over the side of a mountain slope in a limo not long ago. Not to mention the whole wolf-on-her-limo-hood-and-then-abduction-by-a-naked-man event. It was crazy. But she felt so mellow. As if she knew she was safe and everything would be okay.

It had to be the fire. The heat pulsed in waves from the hearth, feeling so delightful against her skin. Listening to the flames crackling and the logs popping was soothing. Watching the flames was mesmerizing.

It was weird because she should've been nervous sitting next to a blazing-hot man like Dalton Kincaid. Even if he hadn't been a wealthy client of the company, she would've been on edge, hoping she didn't embarrass herself by saying or doing something stupid in front of him. She liked to make a good impression.

Unfortunately, she'd already ruined that. She'd actually called him out when he was giving Cole all that grief. Her. Someone hired by Dalton to pick him up and drive him home. She hadn't just stepped over the line, she'd pole vaulted over it.

But this was the weirdest thing. She should have been mortified about it, but she wasn't. She felt comfortable. She felt like she belonged here, with him. With Cole. As if they had known each other and were longtime friends.

Again, weird.

She hadn't been hurt in the crash thanks to the airbag. Not even whiplash or a single bruise. On top of that, she was sitting next to a fire because of Cole's...um, his unconventional invitation. That certainly wasn't something she would ever forget. He'd been naked as the day he'd been born in the middle of a blizzard. Because he was a werewolf, the cold and the nudity hadn't even fazed him. But she wasn't going to forget those strong arms any time soon. Or being wrapped up in a blanket and held close against his warm chest. Almost as warm as the fire…

She shook her head. Tonight felt like a dream. Or a snow day. Maybe a wild vacation, full of possibilities.

Or maybe it was all three. A crazy snow-day-vacation dream. Whatever it was, she was determined to enjoy the warm fire, and the smell of cooking steaks from the cabin's kitchen had her stomach growling.

"I'm glad you weren't hurt in the crash," Dalton said softly.

She stopped staring at the flames, jolted out of her thoughts. "Thank you. So am I actually."

He chuckled. She loved the deep sound of his laughter. It made her feel all tingly in her tummy. She'd never admit that aloud to anyone, not even to Rachel and Deb, her bestest girlfriends.

What would they think of what had happened to her tonight? She couldn't wait to tell them about it over a glass of wine. On second thought, she *could* wait. As much as she'd wanted to get back to town and to safety after the crash, now she just felt…unmotivated. Unmotivated to go anywhere or do anything except stay near this wonderful fire.

"How did the accident happen?" Dalton asked.

She hesitated. "Wind gust. Snowy roads at night. Um. A blizzard."

He gave her a conspiratorial smile. "And you were in a hurry to earn the bonus."

"I..." She stopped. How should she answer that? That had been a factor, but she couldn't admit it. It might get her in trouble with Mirage. She could not lose this job.

"Don't worry," he assured her. "I won't tell. You have my word. Also, I'm still going to pay you the bonus."

Her eyes went wide, and her stomach seemed to drop as if she were on a roller coaster. He was going to pay her the bonus even though they were stuck here right now because of her crash? "You'd do that?"

"Of course I'll do that," Dalton answered. "I know this has been a bit traumatic. Werewolves can be...overwhelming."

He could say that again. But she had the feeling he meant the word "overwhelming" as both a negative and a positive.

And maybe it was.

"Thank you again," she said, truly meaning it. The bonus would make a huge difference in her finances for the next couple of months. It might have been chump change for him, but to her, it was a real life saver. "And thank you for being so easygoing. Not all our clients would be that way."

He grinned at her, his eyes sparkling. "Alpha wolves aren't known for being easygoing, but I get your meaning."

She was quiet for a moment, suddenly very aware of how handsome he was. There was no denying the intensity to him. He was somcone who could walk into a room and have every eye immediately drawn to him. It wasn't even that he'd be wearing the most expensive suit in the room either. He had a power, a charisma, that was hard to deny.

Or to ignore.

She had to stop thinking about him that way. She knew herself well enough to know her own body. And what her body was telling her was how much she was attracted to him. It was clear by her faster heartbeat now that her attention was back on him, how her mouth was dry, and how she kept wanting to lick her lips. How her stomach felt full of butterflies. Not to mention that tightening ache and heat she felt down in her core.

It was mortifying too. Because she suspected that as a werewolf, he could tell how much he turned her on. Maybe he could scent her arousal or tell how flushed her skin was or hear how her heart was pounding. Gone was the calm tranquility that she'd felt while staring at the fire. It had evaporated completely.

Dalton reached out and lifted her necklace from where it lay against the front of her uniform. His eyes narrowed as he examined it. "This is quite pretty. Where did you buy it?"

"I didn't buy it. I...I made it."

"You made this?" He bent a little closer, and she swallowed and took a quick breath. Her body was very aware of his proximity...and wanted to draw him even closer. "I would've sworn it was something from a jeweler."

She flushed at the compliment. God, had he just won her undying admiration with that comment? She suspected he just might have. "Thank you. But you're being too kind. I sometimes like to make jewelry. As a hobby. I'm still learning."

He let go of the necklace and leaned back again. "I'm not being too kind," he said bluntly. "You have talent."

Her heart was pounding even faster now, and her heart suddenly felt like it was full of brilliant sunlight. Cindy tried to reclaim some of her earlier tranquility by focusing on the fireplace again. It might've worked, but

Dalton reached out and took her hand in both of his. His hands were so big and warm. She loved how his skin felt against hers.

She shouldn't be feeling this way. The man was a client of her employer. He was a stranger. He was also an alpha werewolf. She didn't need a bossy shifter in her life, beating his chest and being all dominant.

Listen to her. As if a handsome, wealthy man like Dalton Kincaid would ever be interested in a girl like her. A girl who had big hips and thick legs. He was the kind of man who dated models or centerfolds or movie stars. Probably all three at once.

"Listen, Cindy," Dalton said, then paused. "May I call you Cindy? I know you gave Cole that honor earlier, but I feel it's necessary to ask for me."

She nodded, biting her lip. It was a bad habit she did when she was really nervous. Her hands were sweaty. He could probably tell. How embarrassing to have sweaty palms at a time like this.

"And please call me Dalton," he continued. He looked deep into her eyes with an intensity and focus that not only had her palms sweaty but sent a cold trickle of sweat running down her back. "Tell me the truth. Did Cole attack you?"

She pulled her hand out of his. He let her go,

though she could sense he didn't like it. He didn't say anything, only waiting patiently on her answer. She got the feeling he would wait forever until she told him what he wanted to know.

"No," she answered. She paused, thinking back. "I was afraid. He showed up as a wolf. Then he was naked." Her cheeks heated a little. "I mean, I'm not afraid of naked men. I'm not like…a nun or anything."

God, she sounded utterly stupid. Maybe she could blame it on a concussion.

She pressed on. "I was shaken up by the crash. He wanted me to go with him, but I was afraid."

Dalton nodded. "You certainly can't be blamed for that."

"He only wanted to help though. But he had a strange way of showing it. I mean, maybe he doesn't get many guests, so his bedside manner is lacking. Because he kind of ripped apart the limo…"

"Alphas don't really have any bedside manner," Dalton said, chuckling softly. "We see the best course of action and we take it." He tilted his head, still looking at her closely. "I was shocked when you burst out of the house, yelling for help. I just want to make sure you're safe."

"Well, I thought he was kidnapping me. And…he

kind of was. But he never hurt me." She looked at the dancing flames again. "Actually, I was the one who hurt him. With a log to the head."

"I bet that got his attention."

"I think it's probably best to leave it all in the past," she said briskly. "But as to your question, no, he didn't hurt me. He was a gentleman."

"Even though he was a naked werewolf?"

She snorted. "Even though he was a naked werewolf."

Dalton nodded slowly. "I'm glad to hear that."

She glanced at him. She could see in his eyes that he believed her. That made her feel better. She didn't want them fighting again. Especially over her. She wasn't one of those women who got off on having men fight over her.

What was she saying? She'd never had men fighting over her in her life. How would she know how she felt about it?

"I'm happy I got to meet you like this, Cindy," Dalton continued. He gave her that charming grin that could probably tempt birds, cats, and even spring leaves down from the trees. "It certainly has given us a memorable story." That grin widened. "And the storm isn't over yet, so the story isn't over either."

Her heart was pounding fast again. She swallowed and heard her throat make a gulping sound. A very unladylike gulping sound. She glanced at Dalton again. The firelight on his face made him seem even more handsome somehow. She tried to distract herself by focusing on the sounds of Cole working in the kitchen. She could even smell the aroma of cooking food. That delicious scent had her stomach making all kinds of odd gurgling noises.

When she didn't say anything, he didn't seem to be offended. His intense, dark eyes watched her, but she didn't feel like he was judging her. It just felt like he was deeply interested in her. If that was his superpower—making women think he was one hundred and ten percent focused on them as if there was nothing else important in the world—then it had probably gotten him laid time after time.

She could understand why. Even though her brain was warning her to beware of charming and smooth males, either human or shifter, her body was all in, judging from the waves of pleasure and anticipation coursing through her.

"Cindy," he said, the firelight shining on his face, showing off his high cheekbones, perfect nose, strong jaw. "I don't believe in playing games."

She swallowed hard. "Y-you don't?" God, she sounded foolish. She needed to say something witty. "I think they have their place." Crap. That sounded almost snotty. Better pull out of this nosedive with some humor. "I'm rather fond of Trivial Pursuit."

The smile on her lips felt like plastic. Had she really just said that to this handsome billionaire? Had she really gone there?

Yes. Yes, she had.

Was it too late to melt into a puddle and evaporate out of the room? Because right now she was pretty sure she was beet-red with embarrassment.

Dalton was a gentleman though. He threw her a lifeline by chuckling at her humor-challenged joke. He even did it in such a way that he acknowledged her clumsy stab at being funny without overreacting by falling off the couch with fake laughter that would only make her feel worse.

"If you like that game," he said, his voice low and deep but a smile still tilting up the corners of his lips, "I'll have to play it with you sometime. I'm terrible at it. But what I mean is that I don't play games with relationships. I don't have time. I have businesses to run and a pack to lead."

She nodded her head as if she had the faintest idea

where this was leading. Because she didn't.

He leaned closer to her, but he didn't touch her. Even so, her body sparked with reaction.

"I'm not being clear, am I? My point is, I find you very attractive. I'm not trying to put you on the spot or pressure you. But I want you to know that werewolves had strong reactions to…" He paused, still staring deep into her eyes. She could see he was reaching for the right words. Right now she could barely hear him over the thunder of her own heart. "Strong attractions to males or females who would make outstanding partners." As soon as he said the last word, he suddenly burst out laughing and shook his head. "Listen to me. I sound like a damn businessman."

She tried to get her breath back. Everything was moving so fast. She couldn't believe this was happening. It was like some kind of vibrator-powered fantasy of hers come to life. She would've pinched herself to make sure she was awake, but who actually did that in real life?

"I…" she said wisely. "I…I'm… You're very handsome. And I can't thank you enough for jumping in to defend me. That…was very brave."

Would he kiss her now? She parted her lips a little, just in case. From the heat in his eyes, he was definitely considering it. Kisses, maybe more. A hot surge of lust burst from her core and shuddered through her body. Oh God, she wanted him to touch her. She wanted him, and she wanted Cole…

Wait. That was crazy. Had she turned into some kind of greedy sex glutton? Why would her lust-hazed brain suddenly start thinking of both Dalton and Cole?

In the end, Dalton didn't kiss her, but his charming smile still nearly evaporated her panties.

"Like I said, I'm glad we're getting to spend this time together." Dalton got off the couch. "I should go see how our host is doing. From the aroma, he might actually be good at grilling steaks." He smiled and gave her a wink so quick she wasn't sure she really saw it. "If we leave him alone for too long with the food, I'm afraid we might not get any. Stay here and stay warm. I'll be right back."

She nodded, biting her bottom lip. She watched him saunter to the kitchen. Actually, she watched his butt saunter to the kitchen, since that tight ass practically screamed: "Look at me, Cindy!"

When he vanished into the kitchen, she turned back to the fireplace. The red coals and embers were so pretty. She could lose herself just watching them. They were the perfect thing to stare at as her brain replayed what had just happened. Replayed it over and over and over again.

More than ever, she felt as if today was turning into something special. Something almost magical. A day when anything could happen.

She just had to be bold enough to take advantage of the magic.

CHAPTER FIVE

Dalton

He should have kissed her. His wolf had been all for it. He'd been all for it too. Or at least the constant male lust part of him had definitely been all for it. But in his heart, he knew he'd made the right choice to hold off.

These days, he liked to make it clear to any man or woman he was romantically interested in exactly where he was coming from. That way they could tell him to get lost if they didn't return the affection. He hadn't been lying. He *was* a busy man. He really didn't have time for games.

So perhaps he had been too blunt, making it sound too much like a business deal. And damn, it had been hard to keep himself from sweeping her into his arms and claiming those lips of hers. It had been difficult not to press his body against her lush curves and show her exactly how badly he wanted her.

He *would* kiss her. Tonight. He would claim his mate for his own before Cole could lay his own claim. So yes, he should have kissed her when they'd been alone in front of the fire, but this was part of his plan too. Drawing out the anticipation. Pushing the stakes higher. When he finally kissed her, he wanted his pretty little human practically begging for it. He wanted her sopping wet with desire for him, her breath shuddering out of those plump lips, wanted her hips arching toward him, desperate for his touch. And he would touch her. Oh, how he would touch her.

He grinned as he pushed into the kitchen, his cock straining against his ski pants again. He didn't even give a damn if Cole noticed it. Let the bastard know what he'd been up to in the other room with Cindy. He liked the idea of Cole being jealous of the two of them.

In the kitchen, Cole was standing at the big, gas-powered stovetop. He was searing steaks and cooking some stir-fry too. The air was filled with the mouthwatering aroma of grilled meat and frying vegetables. The wolf loved the meat the most, but he wasn't only a predator. He had a refined palate. He enjoyed good food, prepared well.

Judging from the kitchen, it looked like Cole might be a wolf who felt the same about keeping a broader definition of food than only beef.

Either that or the bastard was trying to impress Cindy by trying not to seem to be such a redneck, lone-wolf, mountain-man hermit. Dalton couldn't discount that possibility either.

Cole heard him enter and glanced his way.

"Dalton," he said, his voice neutral.

"Cole," Dalton replied, keeping the same neutral tone.

He thought he might just dislike Cole even more because of his tempting, rugged good looks. No mountain-man hermit deserved to look that good. Jeans and flannel weren't exactly high fashion. But the bastard actually looked good in them.

"*He will make a fine mate,*" Dalton's wolf assured him almost testily. "*Stop thinking so much. Our feelings are true.*"

He gritted his teeth, suppressing a growl. Now the damn wolf part of him was actually making sense and sounding wise. What was this world coming to?

Right now he was only going to pursue his feelings for Cindy. Cole was not part of that picture. What did his wolf believe? That they would have a fun little threesome and have a happy little life together?

That was crazy. And not just because he and Cole had already fought each other once over Cindy. Sure it had been a misunderstanding, but still. Fighting was fighting.

Cole glanced his way again, watching him with half-lidded eyes. He seemed to sense Dalton's turmoil. Maybe he was even feeling some of his own turmoil.

"How's Cindy?" Cole asked, turning his attention back to the steaks.

"You worried about her?"

Cole frowned. "Yeah."

Fair enough. Maybe he could respect that. A little anyway. "She's warming right up."

That only made Dalton remember how he should've kissed her and warmed her up even more. True, he'd wanted to prove himself a gentleman. He'd wanted to show her that he wasn't the kind of wolf who manhandled people. But now he was increasingly certain he'd missed an opportunity, which wasn't like him.

He bet Cole would've gone for it. The bastard.

Already he hated this guy.

And he wanted him. Because his cock hadn't calmed down since he'd sauntered in here. It should've, given how on edge he was. But he was still rock hard.

Cole turned the steaks again. "What about you? How's the jaw?"

Dalton grunted, touching the sore spot on his jaw where Cole had landed a punch. "Fine. How's your face? I think my fist introduced itself a few times."

Cole chuckled. "Did it? Honestly, I didn't notice."

Oh, what a bastard this guy was. That irked him to the core. He took a deep breath. Cindy had been giving Dalton warning glances earlier when he'd been a bit of a jerk to Cole, so he guessed she wouldn't be thrilled if the two of them started brawling again and burned all the food. It was amazing that he even cared what Cindy thought. As an alpha shifter, he shouldn't care what humans thought. But with her, he did.

Damn it all. This mates thing was a royal pain in his ass.

"I'm not going to apologize for fighting with you out there," Dalton growled. "So if you're waiting for that, you'll be waiting a long time."

Cole snorted. "I wasn't exactly holding my breath."

Dalton crossed his arms and leaned against the counter as he eyed Cole. Time to be blunt. "I'm making my claim on her. This is your one warning."

Cole didn't answer. He didn't even look at Dalton. But it wasn't a submissive thing. It was as if he didn't think Dalton's words were even worth a response.

"You hear me?" Dalton pressed, his fists clenching. If this other wolf didn't acknowledge him and his claim, there was going to be trouble.

"I heard you," Cole replied. Then he grinned and shrugged. "But you're too late. I already made my claim when I rescued her from the crash. What were you doing? Oh, that's right. You were skiing."

Dalton was across the kitchen in an instant, fists clenched. "You didn't rescue anybody. You frightened her half to death. I'm glad she clobbered you with a piece of firewood. You fucking deserved it."

Calmly, Cole took the steaks off the heat and turned down the temperature on the vegetable stir-fry. He looked at Dalton, his ice-blue eyes narrowing dangerously.

"If I deserved it," Cole said, his baritone as cold as the snow outside, "then that's between her and me. Not you. My wolf has been telling me she's my mate since the moment I caught her scent." He crossed his arms, his biceps bulging. "I'm not going to apologize for doing everything I can to keep my mate safe."

Dalton froze. So this jerk was claiming Cindy as his mate? Usually that would've sent Dalton's wolf into a possessive rage. But strangely, only the human side of him seemed angered by it. The wolf only seemed to accept it.

"Because he is our mate too," his wolf insisted, sounding oddly long-suffering. As if the human side of Dalton was a hopeless dumbass. *"She is our mate. He is our mate. We are three."*

Dalton knew little about such things, honestly. He'd heard of werewolves and shifters having multiple mates, even being happy with such an arrangement, but he'd never once believed it might happen to him. Cindy as a mate, he could understand. She was just the type of female he preferred. Curvaceous, vivacious, with a little sass and a lot to love. She struck him as the kind of woman who could go the distance in bed. Regrettably, he didn't have any concrete evidence of that—not yet anyway—but he intended to change that.

But he couldn't understand this Cole guy. He liked fucking guys just as much as he liked fucking women, but the guys he was drawn toward were in the same general social circles. Well-to-do guys who were comfortable in a suit and tie. Cole looked like he'd never worn anything but flannel and blue jeans in his entire life. Dalton didn't want to be an elitist about it, but he couldn't fool himself either. He didn't understand where this was all coming from. Why was Dalton's wolf claiming this loner wolf living out in the wilderness? They had nothing in common. In fact, they were practically enemies.

He realized he was growling low in his throat. He stopped, but he still narrowed his eyes at Cole, taking another threatening step toward the man. "She's not your mate. She's mine. I was the one who hired her."

"I'm going to repeat myself because you aren't listening. *I* was the one who saved her after you made her come all the way out to the Rocky Mountains at night during the worst blizzard of the year."

"You son of a bitch," Dalton snarled.

Cole stepped toward him. "Hey, that's *my* line."

Enough. He was alpha of the Granite Hill Pack. He wasn't going to take this insolence from some crazy lone wolf who was poaching on Dalton's territory. Cindy belonged to him. When he kissed her, she would be thinking of Dalton, not Cole. When he made her come, her body shuddering around him, she would call his name, not Cole's. This bastard needed to be taught a lesson. Dalton didn't have time to be a gentleman about it either. His alpha instincts roared to the surface.

It was lesson-teaching time.

He raised his fist, ready to fight. But Cole caught his forearm in a grip like steel.

Dalton tensed, ready to dodge the counter-attack and ready to yank his arm free.

Instead of attacking him, Cole did something completely unexpected.

Cole dragged him forward until they pressed up against each other, body to body. Before Dalton could shove him away, Cole seized him by the back of the head, twisting his fingers in Dalton's hair and drawing his head back. Tilting his mouth to the perfect angle…

Then Cole captured Dalton's lips with his own.

The kiss had him reeling. The desire to fight instantly vanished. It was replaced by true desire. He growled low and fiercely in his throat, but it was a sound of need.

He wrapped his arms around Cole in a tightening embrace as he kissed Cole back with even more intensity. Part of him wanted to kiss this other rival wolf into submission. The rest of him just wanted their kiss to go on and on forever…

His body was out of his control, consumed with

the sudden flare of his need. He ground his hips forward, pressing his hard cock against Cole's muscular body.

To his delight, Cole pumped his hips in return. A primal thrill went through Dalton when he realized he could feel Cole's erection through the jeans he was wearing.

Cole deepened the kiss even more. Dalton's hand came up and rested on Cole's chest, feeling the tight chest muscle beneath his palm. Feeling the pounding of the other man's heart. Inside Dalton's head, his wolf howled its joy to be touching one of its mates. Dalton wasn't able to think, only to feel. Only to give in to this torrent of desire rushing through him.

Dalton realized he had to regain the upper hand. Right now. So he deepened the kiss and thrust his tongue into Cole's mouth. He plundered Cole's mouth, and the other shifter's tongue met Dalton's, and a groan of desire escaped Cole's lips.

Behind them, the door swung open. Both of them clearly heard Cindy's gasp.

They immediately broke apart from their embrace. Dalton spun to face her, stepping away from Cole. Meanwhile, Cole leaned back against the counter, a self-satisfied grin on his face.

The cocky bastard.

"Oh, I'm so sorry," Cindy said, a bright red flush filling her cheeks. "I didn't know… I didn't mean to interrupt. If… I mean…excuse me. I was, um, wondering if the food was ready…"

Her gaze dropped down, seemingly against her will, to Dalton's crotch, then skipped over to Cole's groin. She sucked in a breath, and he heard her sudden swallow. He knew his erection was outlined against his pants, clear to see and bold as day. Cole's hard-on was just as easy to see in his jeans, his long cock throbbing down his right leg, pinned against his thigh. Her eyes were wide, and she looked away quickly as if trying not to be caught staring.

God, she was so genuine and unscripted. He loved it. He was used to men and women using all kinds of guile on him to get what they wanted—and what they usually wanted was his money. But she didn't seem to have a deceitful bone in her body. Every emotion seemed to flash in her eyes and across her face, making her easy to read. But he had the advantage of being able to read her scent too. Right now she was flustered, a mix between the heady scent of her feminine arousal and the smell of her embarrassment having caught them tongue-fucking each other.

Cole chuckled. Dalton wasn't going to lie. The

sound of that chuckle sent an erotic thrill through his whole body, tightening his balls and making his hard cock twitch.

"No need to apologize, sweetheart," Cole drawled. He tilted his head to the side as he gazed at her. "Dalton here was just trying to make up with me. He felt bad that I bruised my knuckles on his face. I told him it's quite all right." A slow grin crossed his rugged face. "Well, that was the message I was trying to give him anyway."

Dalton shook his head, throwing a dark look at the other shifter before turning his attention back to her. "It's not like that, Cindy."

But he could see how her mind changed once the shock of seeing them in each other's arms began to wear off. She didn't believe him. Worse, he could see he was losing ground with her. All the ground he'd gained just minutes ago out on the couch by the fire.

She stepped back and put her hand on the kitchen door. "Uh. Okay. I mean…it's cool. I just…was surprised." She tried a smile, which looked as fake as a Loch Ness monster hoax. "Um. I'll leave you alone and go put another log on the fire. Tell me when the food's ready, please."

With that, she bolted through the door, back out

into Cole's living room. The door swung shut. For a moment, they both stood there staring at it.

Dalton closed his eyes, leaning his head back with a groan. Why the hell had he even come in here? That's right. To check on the food, but mostly to tell Cole to keep his paws off Dalton's mate.

How the hell had he ended up kissing Cole? And then being caught by Cindy? It was a complete disaster.

"She looks like a startled horse," Cole said. "I'll go to her."

"The hell you will," Dalton snarled. "We'll both go to her."

Cole smirked at him, his blue eyes flashing with amusement. "Afraid I'll steal her for myself?"

"I told you. She's mine."

But Cole only kept grinning. "Guess we'll see about that."

CHAPTER SIX

Cole

He had no regrets about hauling off and kissing the hell out of Dalton. The other alpha had been asking for it. He'd been begging for either a punch in the mouth...or a kiss on the lips. Cole had gone with the second option. Like he'd said, he didn't regret it either. Not for an instant.

But he didn't want Cindy feeling like a third wheel either. Especially because whenever Cole thought of her, he couldn't help but imagine kissing her deeply. He wanted to hold her tight, feeling her body pressed up against his. She was not only pretty and tempting, but she had a fire that he'd definitely come to like. Yeah, that fire was annoying when it meant she was stubbornly refusing to leave her limo, but it also gave her a spark of life that lit up any room she was in.

He had to have her in his life. There it was. Plain and simple.

Dalton, now, that was a different story, scorching-hot kiss or no. Sexy little grind-fest or no. The guy was one of those wealthy alphas used to getting his own way. There were a few reasons Cole preferred to remain a lone wolf out here in the middle of nowhere. He didn't have to put up with alphas like Dalton, giving orders and asserting dominance.

Cole pushed through the kitchen door, stepping into the living room with Dalton right behind him. He smirked. Dalton was so territorial. It might have been endearing if it hadn't been so damn irritating. Maybe Cole should kiss him again, and then when the guy was still dazed from the kiss, he would clock him on the chin and knock him on his ass. Teach the rich alpha a lesson.

But now wasn't the time for that. Right now, Cole had to do a little damage control. His wolf insisted the little human was his mate. But the damn-fool wolf also insisted Dalton was his mate. And that had led to the kiss. And that had led to Cindy finding them and getting the wrong idea.

Or the *right* idea…

Still, he had to set things straight and fast.

Cindy was pacing in front of the fire. His heart immediately went out to her because she looked so distraught. Now he started to feel a little guilt. He didn't want her upset. He wanted to make her smile. He wanted to make her sigh with pleasure. He wanted to keep her safe and protected and happy. Making her upset was not part of the mission plan.

He went to her, shouldering Dalton aside when Mr. Money Bags tried to get to Cindy first. Dalton grunted…and even though he bared his teeth, he didn't make a move to stop Cole as he stepped in front of Cindy. He took both of Cindy's hands, looking down into her earnest face. Her eyes were so big and wide. They were beautiful. What was the saying? Something about falling into a woman's eyes and drowning there? That didn't seem like such a bad fate after all.

"You're upset," he murmured to her. Her hands felt very warm from the fireplace heat. He loved how they felt in his grip. Small, warm, her skin smooth as satin. "Talk to me."

"I'm not upset," Cindy replied quickly. "I mean, who would be upset seeing two hot men making out?"

She laughed nervously.

He gave her a reassuring smile, still looking deep into her eyes. He needed her to believe him because every word he would say to her was going to be the truth. He would never lie to his mate. It was crazy to even begin accepting that she was his mate…but this close to her, he couldn't deny it either. The power she had over him was staggering.

"We were caught up in the moment. It happens with wolves," he said. "But do you want to know why Dalton was in the kitchen with me? Do you want to know what we were talking about before you found us?"

Dalton threw him a warning look. Clearly, Dalton didn't want him to jump into the whole "mate" thing or talk about the claim they'd both made on her. He was no fool. If he did this wrong, Cindy was likely to run off into the snowstorm again…or go after another blunt object like the firewood.

But still, she deserved to know how Cole felt about her. Why he'd been so determined to get her somewhere safe, even if it meant wrapping her in a blanket and carrying her off. That had been a primal urge to protect her that was too powerful to deny.

Cindy bit her lip, glancing from him to Dalton and back again. God, he wanted to drag her into his arms and kiss the hell out of her. There was no denying it. The urge was that powerful. His little mate. His curvy, big and beautiful mate. His desire was so intense it was almost painful.

After a pause, she finally gave him a hesitant answer. "You were talking about...steak?"

Both Cole and Dalton burst out laughing.

"A good guess," Dalton said, his voice low, deep, and amused.

"I agree one-hundred percent," Cole added. "That was a good guess. With werewolves, half the time we're talking about dinner." He shook his head, turning serious again. "But no, beautiful. We were talking about *you*."

Her cheeks flushed pink. She looked away and withdrew her hands from his. He let her go, though it killed him a little to give up touching her.

"You shouldn't call me beautiful," she said, her voice barely above a whisper. "And why were you talking about me?"

Dalton reached out and put a hand on her shoulder. It was more of a comforting gesture than a romantic one. Cole could sense that it eased her a little. Calmed her. It seemed the alpha wolf was good for something at least.

Well, something besides kissing.

"Cole's only telling the truth," Dalton said. "You *are* beautiful. I'm not going to let you sell yourself short." He glanced at Cole. Cole nodded to him. Dalton continued. "It looks like Cole feels the same as I do. Neither of us will let you undermine yourself. You're beautiful to us. End of story."

His tone brooked no argument. Even Cole, as rebellious and stubborn as he could be, felt his wolf accept this. Maybe because it was one of his mates saying it. Maybe simply because it was true. She was beautiful and special. End of story.

If he thought about it too much, it might drive him to do something rash. Dalton had already stirred his blood. It had been a hell of a night so far. Fighting, kissing, storms. Throw in some hot food and some wild sex and tonight would be damn well perfect.

Cindy watched them both, seeming unsure what to say. He could hear her heart beating quickly. Her scent told him she was a tangle of emotions. It was difficult for him to sort them out, so he didn't try. He intended to get some hot food in her. That would calm everything down. Especially when emotions were running hot.

He gave her his most charming smile. He was a bit out of practice, living out here on his own and not seeing folks very often. But these were his guests, and he'd been raised to show western hospitality. Besides, he was having fun. It surprised him to realize that, because before these two had crashed into his life, he'd thought himself largely done with humans and other shifters alike. He wasn't any curmudgeon or people-hater. It was just that out here away from civilization, he could be himself. And he could be his wolf.

That was what it really came down to. That was the reason why he would never settle down and live a suburbs life. Well, that and the fact that he'd never found his mate, so it wasn't an issue.

Until now, if what his wolf was telling him was true. And it wasn't just one mate but two.

"I know Dalton will be happy to tell you exactly why we were talking about you," Cole said cheerfully. "But we should do it over dinner. Now give me a chance to plate up the food, and I'll bring it out, and we can scarf it down."

"Out here?" Dalton asked. "Don't you have a dining room table?"

Cole glanced at him. "Eating in the living room next to a roaring fire is the best thing ever."

One of Dalton's eyebrows slowly rose. "So…you don't eat at the table then?"

"You know what I use my dining room table for?" Cole shot back. "Somewhere to sort mail."

Cindy laughed. The sound was like music to his ears. He excused himself, walking toward the kitchen to serve up the food.

"What would you like to drink?" he called over his shoulder. "I have beer, soda, or bottled water."

"No wine?" Dalton asked.

Cole halted and looked at him, keeping his face neutral. "Afraid not. Although you could put some grapes in your beer and pretend if you're of mind."

Cindy spoke up quickly. "I'll have a beer, thanks!"

"Me as well," Dalton finally added, choosing to let the wine comment go.

"Three beers then." Cole headed through the door into the kitchen. The food wasn't at the perfect temperature anymore because of all the distractions, but it still smelled delicious. His mouth was already watering.

He took the food out to his guests and even set up TV trays for them at the couch near the fire. He might live alone, but the TV tray holder he'd assembled had come with four on a stand…so that seemed like fate, right?

"I've never eaten on a TV tray," Dalton said,

staring at his tray as Cole put his plate of food on it. From his expression, he looked like he was being asked to eat on the bottom of an upside-down garbage can.

"Don't be such a fuddy-duddy," Cindy chided. "Cole's right. This is the best. We get to eat right next to the beautiful fire."

Cole grinned and winked at Dalton, reveling in his little victory. Dalton snorted and dropped the subject. Cole was determined to get the rich alpha to pull out at least part of that snobby stick he had up his ass. This seemed like a good first step.

Cindy was already digging in. "This is so good." She took another forkful. "Like fancy-steakhouse good!"

"Thank you," he replied, pleased she liked it.

Dalton took his time chewing. Then he nodded, throwing a curious look Cole's way. "It's good. Where did you learn to grill like this?"

"The Marines. Barbecue's a big thing. Spent a lot of time over the coals."

"Oh!" Cindy said. "My dad's a Marine. He's going to love you! He loved barbecues even more than football."

Good deal. He couldn't have planned that more perfectly. From the look on Dalton's face, the other alpha was aware that Cole was edging ahead. Not that this was a race or a competition…

Okay, that was a lie. With alpha wolves, *everything* was a competition. But it was one he intended to win. It had been a long time since he'd had to compete in this game, but it thrilled him that he hadn't lost a step.

"So," Dalton said to him. "You live out here alone. Like a hermit."

Cole frowned. He could guess where Dalton was going with this. Even though part of him wanted to kiss the man again and relive that incredible moment, the rest of him was irked by his attitude.

"Is that so strange?" Cole asked. "You city shifters have lost touch with your wolves."

"Boys," Cindy said, putting a hand on each of them. "Can we not? Please? Not too long ago I walked in on the two of you kissing. Now you're back at it again." She shook her head, frowning. "What in God's name is wrong with werewolves?"

Cole chuckled. He loved how she spoke her mind. He didn't care for demure, passive women. He wanted a spitfire. No wonder he liked her. She wasn't obnoxious, brash, and abrasive, but she didn't bite her tongue either. She spoke her mind with confidence.

He respected that.

"What's wrong with werewolves?" Cole mused.

"That's a long story. Mostly it has to do with fancy city wolves losing touch with their true selves. A wolf can't be cut off from nature."

Dalton glared at him. "What are you talking about? Do you have a concussion or something? Did you forget that I hired Cindy to pick me up after I skied down a mountain? I don't know if you can get much closer to nature than that."

Cole shrugged. "Did you do it as a wolf?"

"A wolf on skis would make for an interesting ski run," Dalton snapped.

Cindy burst out laughing. Cole immediately felt his ire fading some. Her laughter was soothing to him.

God, listen to him right now. He'd lived alone out here for half a decade, ever since he'd gotten out of the Marines and his father had passed on and willed the place to him. He'd been happy. He'd been at peace. But now he began to suspect something had been missing. Like the sound of laughter from a woman he cared for. Or the kiss from a man he desired. Or simply sharing food in the warmth of a fire as a storm raged outside, but they were in inside, safe and sound.

"Fair enough," Cole finally answered Dalton's quip with a wide grin. "Aside from that, there's nothing wrong with werewolves. We even look good naked."

That got the right response from both of them, easing the tension. Dalton smirked. Cindy was obviously remembering seeing him in the buff because her pupils widened, her heart rate jumped, and he caught her biting her bottom lip. She covered it well, but being a shifter gave him certain advantages.

Besides, women were mysterious enough. A guy needed all the help he could get.

Cindy recovered quickly, he'd give her that. She gave him a coy look. "So does that mean you live out here alone so you can be naked whenever you want?"

Dalton replied before Cole could answer. "Lone wolves don't fit in with packs all that well. They're alpha, but they don't want the obligation of the pack."

"Or the politics and problems and backstabbing," Cole added. "I followed orders in the military, but nowadays, I'm one hundred percent my own man." He glanced at Cindy. "My father gave me this land after he passed."

"I'm sorry to hear he's passed," she said. "But he left you something wonderful."

He nodded, not even trusting himself to smile. She'd said just about the perfect thing that could be said to him. This place was wonderful. He wouldn't trade it for the world.

"What do you do for a living?" Dalton asked him suddenly, his stare intense. "Now that you're out of the service?"

Cole refused to be shamed or intimidated by Dalton's questions, tone, or stare. That was one of the problems with pack alphas: everything they did seemed designed to establish and keep dominance. It annoyed him. If his wolf hadn't kept insisting Dalton was one of their mates...and if not for that kiss, he would've kicked Dalton out on his ass. That was what he thought of pack alphas.

"I mostly work as a ranch hand when the work is available. Or as a handyman to a few people I know around here." He shrugged. "I have a bit saved up from my time in uniform." His mouth curved in a smile. "I work to keep busy and keep the calluses on my hands. Honest work is good for the soul. That's what mama always said."

"I respect that," Dalton said with a nod.

Cole had to wonder when the last time a rich guy like Dalton got his hands dirty, but he let it go. Cindy had told them to cool it. Besides, kissing Dalton had been more fun than punching him. Now if he could just get his lips on Cindy, everything would be perfect.

Cindy turned to Dalton with a sparkle in her eye.

"Cole's told us about himself. Now what about you?"

"Ladies first," Dalton replied with a grin.

She took a deep breath. "Fine. But prepare to be bored to death. And remember, you asked for it!"

Grinning, Cole took a sip from his beer before throwing another couple of logs on the fire. He didn't want any distractions or interruptions. She deserved his entire focus. He wanted to know what she liked, her thoughts, fears, dreams, her past and what she hoped for the future.

In short, he wanted to know everything about her. Right now, with his belly full, a beer in hand, and the heat from the fire radiating against him, he thought it just about the perfect time for stories.

CHAPTER SEVEN

Cindy

She didn't know where to start. Her life was certainly nothing special. She had good parents she loved, though they lived far away in Texas, and she missed spending holidays with them. She was a chauffeur. She liked to eat cereal at night when watching movies. She had some close girlfriends that she loved, Rachel and Deb. She hadn't done that well in college. Once she finally moved out of her no-pet apartment, she was going to buy a dog to spoil. For a hobby, she liked to fool around making jewelry. Yawn city.

Maybe she could make exciting something up. She

could be a plus-sized Wonder Woman with bullet-proof wrist guards. Or better yet, she could be a super spy, like a female Bond, with a harem of sexy men and a mission to save the world!

No, no one was going to believe that.

She might as well get this out of the way so she could go back to listening to Cole and Dalton talking about themselves again. She was fascinated by both of them. She wasn't the kind of person who liked to sit around talking about herself.

"I'm just a small-town girl from Texas. Um, San Antonio specifically. I work for Mirage Confidential as a chauffeur…which you probably guessed. I know, breaking news!" She smiled sheepishly. "I moved to Colorado after my second year in college because I wanted to make my way in the world." She raised her hands in a half shrug. "How boring, right? I guess I'm still trying to find my way in life."

"There's nothing wrong with that," Dalton said, leaning forward and resting his elbows on his knees.

She met his gaze. She probably should've let that one lie, but she couldn't. Still, she kept a smile on her face as she teased him. "Oh really? When did *you* make your first million, Mr. Dalton Kincaid?"

He rubbed his chin as he held her stare. "Believe it

or not, I don't really like to talk about money. For me, it's just a tool."

Cole leaned back in his chair, stretched out and crossed his legs. "Must be nice. For the rest of us, it's how we can afford to eat."

Dalton looked uncomfortable. She immediately felt bad for him. She had only been teasing him after all. She didn't want to rich-shame him. Although that seemed like a pretty strange and laughable thing to be arguing about. It did remind her that she was here because he'd hired Mirage to pick him up at the bottom of the mountain. She'd been so thrilled at the chance of a bonus. Now she was just hoping to keep her job after wrecking the limo in a storm.

She pushed that thought aside. She didn't want worries to ruin her night. Especially because she was feeling great right now. The meal had been hot and tasty. She was safe and warm. And she had two handsome gentlemen with her. Of course, she now knew they were gay because of the whole kiss thing she'd walked in on. The kiss that had dropped her jaw open as she'd practically soaked her panties. She hadn't realized that two men locked in such a passionate kiss could be so damn hot!

But it was also a mixed blessing. She'd been sure

Dalton was flirting with her earlier. And the same with Cole. She hadn't realized she had such a huge, raging ego. She had misread the whole thing. She should've known. In a way, it soothed her nerves a little. These two men might be very different from each other, but they were both so handsome it was a bit unsettling. Now she could admire the man candy without having to worry about choosing between them.

That was a good thing, right?

Right?

But then, what had they meant when they'd told her they had been talking about her? Why had they insisted she was beautiful? Why was she getting so many mixed and confusing signals?

She knew she should keep making small talk so she didn't have to think about her non-existent love life or how she'd completely misread the signals from not one but both of these two wolves.

Besides, she might drive wealthy shifters around Colorado, but she didn't know what it would be like to actually fall in love with one. Sure, on the surface it sounded sexy-hot and perfect, but sometimes looks could be deceiving. Right now she just wanted a bit of fantasy to keep her spirits high.

"Oh, I almost forgot," she said. "I like to make

jewelry. For a hobby."

"Really?" Cole said, his hands laced behind his head, but his eyes sharp as he looked at her. "I wish I had a creative bone in my body. Do you have anything you've made that I can see?"

Maybe he won her heart right then, like Dalton had earlier. It certainly felt like it as a thrill rushed through her. She was excited to show him...and shy about showing off. She hoped he liked it. She knew she had a smidge of talent, but she was grateful that he was showing any interest at all. Even though her friends and parents and coworkers all praised her creations, she still felt hesitant and self-conscious about her hobby.

She took out the necklace she'd made with hands that trembled a little. She tilted the pendant so the malachite and silver shone in the firelight. "I made this."

Cole got out of his seat so he could look at the necklace more closely. His big, rough hands touched hers gently as he took hold of the necklace and peered at it. She could smell his scent. He smelled of evergreen trees and male. She found herself leaning more closely toward him, smelling him as if she was a wolf herself. The back of her neck grew hot. What was she doing, inhaling his scent like this? It was just...odd. But she couldn't draw away with him so close to her as he examined her necklace.

"It's beautiful," Cole finally said. "I'd love to own something like this."

Her heart began to beat faster, and she could barely contain her pleasure at his praise. He didn't sound like a man just shining her on. He didn't go overboard, proclaiming her the Da Vinci of homemade jewelry, but it was clear he was impressed. His words were simple but heartfelt.

And that meant a lot to her.

"Thank you," she replied, her voice a little shaky.

Then Dalton was leaning in beside her, gently taking the necklace from Cole so he could examine it again. Cole gave it over without protest, and that made her happy. She didn't want them at each other's throats again. She tried not to think about how Dalton had the scent of some fine cologne. Something with Sandalwood? That was her guess. Whatever it was, he smelled just as alluring as Cole did.

It was distracting. So was the way her body was reacting to the both of them. Did she have to draw her body a diagram? Did she have to explain in detail why it was useless drooling over either of them when they liked other men? God, what was wrong with her? She belonged in an asylum.

"Like I said earlier, this is good work," Dalton affirmed.

"Thanks," she murmured, unable to keep the grin from her face. Her skin felt hot enough to make a match head burst into flames, but her spirit was soaring high.

Dalton wasn't looking at her. He was still examining the necklace, turning it in his big fingers. "Have you thought of going into business for yourself? Artisans can make a lot of money in Colorado." He glanced at her. "And then there's online."

"I-I haven't thought about it. That all seems so complex. I wouldn't know where to start."

"Start at the beginning," Dalton said, finally letting the necklace fall back against the front of her chauffeur uniform. "And go from there. I'd be happy to lend you one of my business advisors if you'd like." He waved a hand. "She could help you set up LLCs, tax IDs, put you in contact with some of the vendors. Things like that."

She didn't know what to say. She didn't know why he was making such a generous offer. In fact, she was a little scared to accept it, because doing all that was such a huge change. The biggest change she'd ever made in her life so far was moving away from Texas. Starting her own business? Becoming an artisan? That sounded crazy. It sounded out of her reach.

But he seemed so confident that it was easy. Maybe it was for a businessman like him, but for her, she doubted it would be easy.

"You should take him up on that," Cole urged her quietly.

She glanced over at him and met his beautiful blue eyes. He seemed so earnest. As if her success really mattered to him.

Dalton glanced at Cole, sounding surprised when he said, "I didn't think you'd jump to support one of my ideas."

Cole gave a cocky grin. "That's your alpha wolf, leader-of-the-pack brain talking. It's not 'I win, you lose' or vice versa. This is about Cindy. She has some real talent." He glanced at her, and his smile turned warm. "It's easy to see that her jewelry means a lot to her. So hell yeah, she should go for it."

Hearing them cheer her on made her believe she really could do it. If she could push aside these fears of change and the unknown and take a bold step, then maybe her whole life would open up for her. She didn't need to make a lot of money. Just enough to eat and keep a roof over her head, but if she could do that while also doing something she loved…

That might just be as close to heaven as she ever got.

She put the necklace out of sight again. Her luck seemed to be changing, so she didn't want to jinx it by thinking too hard on the necklace.

Cole began to clear away the plates. She moved to help, but he ordered her to take it easy. He headed into the kitchen with the dishes and to get them all another beer.

Feeling restless, she got up and wandered from the pulsing heat of the fireplace over to the house's front windows. Her body felt a little stiff, a bit sore. Not anything she'd need to see a doctor over, but she knew it was a result of the limo going over the guardrail and hitting a tree. She'd thought she'd got off without a scratch, but now that some time had passed, a few aches were appearing.

Outside, the snow was still falling, but more slowly. The wind had died down too. The night outside looked surprisingly bright. Drifts of snow were piled against the house and blown up against the tree trunks, making her think of the scenes on Christmas cards.

It looked as if the storm was moving on. She wondered if they were worried about her at work yet and realized that was a foolish question. They were probably freaking out. She hadn't checked in on the radio after the accident because of interference from the storm. It wasn't as if they could even get a tow truck up here until the roads were plowed though.

Dalton came up to stand beside her, looking out the window with her. "Beautiful, isn't it?"

"It always seems so magical."

He chuckled. "Different from Texas."

"Sometimes it feels like I'm in a whole different world..."

Cole came striding out of the kitchen with three cold beers. He handed them out and twisted off the cap of his. "Admiring the weather?"

"I was just telling Dalton about how magical it looks out there. This place is stunning."

Cole grinned at her. He looked as pleased about her gushing at the landscape as she'd been about Cole and Dalton complimenting the necklace she'd made.

"Glad you think so," he said. "There's a real upside to living out in the middle of nowhere."

The three of them stood and stared out at the storm. Cole had turned off most of the lights after they'd finished eating to save generator power. The effect on the atmosphere was striking. The room was now almost entirely lit by the mellow orange glow from the fire. The light moved, and the shadows shivered a little as the flames danced and the coals blazed. She felt an ache in her heart at how beautiful it all was.

"What are you thinking right now?" Dalton asked her. He was standing very close to her. His eyes were on her, not the scene out the window.

She surprised herself by telling him exactly how she'd been feeling tonight since she'd met them both. Well...after the rocky introduction to Cole, that was.

"I'm thinking about how this all seems like a wonderful dream." She didn't look at either of them. She kept her gaze on the snow as she took this risk and poured out her feelings. She only prayed they wouldn't laugh at her. "Tonight everything seems too wonderful and special and...rare. Like these events could never happen this way again."

Cole was watching her curiously, but when she risked a glance his way, he looked as if he understood. He rubbed his chin, frowning as he considered her words. "I've never been one for fancy words, but tonight does seem different." He shook his head, his brow furrowed. "The storm. Meeting you both. It feels like fate."

Dalton nodded thoughtfully. "It might sound a little cheesy when said out loud, but I think you're both right."

Cindy looked at him and then at Cole. The two men shared a meaningful glance as if they knew or understood something she didn't. Maybe it was the kiss they'd shared.

But even if she was an outsider here—the third wheel, the token human—the things that had happened still felt like fate to her. It felt as if this was a once-in-a-lifetime thing. Almost like Cinderella's night at the ball. But in Cindy's case, she was sure there would be no prince chasing her down as his true love afterward, trying to fit her foot into a glass slipper.

But that didn't mean she couldn't enjoy what life threw her way. She could wallow in worries and fears of what came next but why waste the emotional energy? She was safe. She was warm. She couldn't leave because of the storm. Tomorrow she would deal with all the problems that were waiting for her. Tomorrow she'd leave Cole behind at his cabin in the Rockies. Tomorrow Dalton would become just another billionaire she was paid to drive around to the ski towns. But for right now, she didn't want this magical, anything-could-happen feeling to end.

Too bad she already knew she wasn't going to get a perfect night. After all, she'd already tricked herself into thinking Dalton and Cole had been flirting with her when they'd really been interested in each other all along. But still, that was what her heart wanted. Maybe it was greedy, but she was only human. She wanted to be happy too…

Listen to her. She really was greedy, wanting something she couldn't have. How could she forget that look the two men had shared seconds ago? So much for her stupid feelings about how this was some kind of fate, some kind of fairy tale. She *was* the outsider. She was just a girl too wide in the hips, too big in the bust, too thick in the thighs and upper arms to ever show up on those magazine covers in the grocery store check-out line. She was only a chauffeur, not some wealthy, sophisticated heiress that Dalton might court. She wasn't even some wild cowgirl in boots and denim that Cole might chase.

Assuming, of course, that they hadn't been gay, which the kiss of theirs that she'd stumbled upon proved beyond a doubt.

Cindy turned away from the beautiful view of the falling snow. She needed to get a handle on these emotions spinning inside her. She wanted that simple happiness she'd been feeling only seconds ago to come back.

But as she took a step back toward her spot near

the fire, Dalton caught her hand. His grip was gentle but firm. His touch seemed to set her body on fire from the inside out, rocking her with raw desire. Her nipples went tight and hard, her pussy muscles clenched, and her mouth suddenly felt bone dry. She silently cursed her body for reacting to him so strongly. It only made everything more difficult. It hurt to want something she couldn't have.

"Cindy," Dalton said. "About earlier. When you surprised us in the kitchen—"

She gave a dismissive shake of her head. "Oh, I'm sorry I interrupted. I didn't know you two..."

Cole reached out and took her other hand. His fingers and palms were rough and calloused from work. She froze, her heart jumping into her mouth. With both of them touching her and both of them focused on her so intently, she felt like her brain might explode with a tornado of sex hormones. That was the least romantic way she could describe it, but that was exactly what she felt like right now. Nothing as refined-sounding as "a sweet tempest of desire" or "a coursing river of need flowing through her flesh," but a straight-up hormone sex tornado explosion in her body.

All the same, she was never going to say those phrases out loud. To anyone. Ever. Not even her best girlfriends.

"No apologies needed," Cole told her emphatically. "In fact, we promised to talk to you about this over dinner, and then the conversation went its own way. We need to talk about us. It's not a coincidence that the three of us met."

"What? I don't..." Was he implying that this blizzard was fate or that her crash was destiny? Because that was crazy.

"He's right," Dalton said. "The first time I saw you..." He paused, then pressed on. "The first time my wolf caught your scent, I couldn't deny it. You're my mate." He lifted her hand to his lips and kissed her skin tenderly, then he glanced at Cole and frowned. "Of course, this jerk had to show up and complicate things."

Her head was spinning. Did he just say *mate*? She knew werewolves believed they could find their true soulmates and they would be happy together forever. Was that what Dalton was claiming? That...that she was his mate in that way? But their kiss... Was he just messing with her?

She yanked her hand out of his grip and turned away. Tears blurred her eyes. Emotion swelled, tightening her throat until it was difficult to breathe. She practically stumbled her way back to the couch.

She didn't want to look at them. She didn't want them to see the hurt in her eyes. She didn't know why Dalton was toying with her, but it was cruel.

Cole was at her side in an instant. There was real dismay on his rugged face. "Cindy, what's wrong? Talk to me."

She looked down at the fire, blinking quickly and trying to get her emotions under control. "I don't appreciate being toyed with. I might be human, but I'm not an idiot. You were kissing Dalton. That's fine. That's great. I wish you all the happiness in the world. But don't make up stories that you think I'm beautiful or I'm some kind of mate—"

Her words stopped when Cole put his hands on her shoulders, leaned in, and captured her lips in a kiss.

She stiffened in surprise. His lips were warm on hers. Her mind went blank, but her body reacted, taking over as her need intensified. She closed her eyes and opened her lips, tempting him into deepening the kiss by sheer instinct. He did, drawing her body closer, right up against his.

When he finally ended the kiss, he drew back slowly. She opened her eyes, looking into his blue gaze. She was trembling slightly. Her thoughts were more tangled than yarn after a cat had been at it.

"I've wanted to do that since I pulled you out of that limo," Cole nearly growled. "I don't like to waste a lot of words. So did that kiss explain things?"

She took a deep breath, feeling her heart racing. She looked deep into his eyes and said, "No."

Dalton laughed. "Cole, that's got to hurt."

"I can't lie," Cole replied, grinning and rubbing his chin. His fingers brushed against his five o'clock shadow, making a rasping sound. "It does sting a little."

"This isn't funny," Cindy said. "I meant what I said. Don't toy with me. This isn't a game for me."

"No game," Dalton told her, his eyes flashing and his tone serious. "I don't lie. Especially about something as important as a mate. This is *very* important. For both of us."

"I know it sounds like it's coming out of the blue," Cole added. "And I know it sounds strange after you walked in on us in the kitchen."

She looked from him to Dalton, her lips still tingling from the kiss. "But…three?"

Cindy wasn't a prude, but the thought of being loved by two men who also loved each other…it seemed almost decadent, almost like too much of a good thing. Like something that could never be real.

She had no idea how that would work in real life.

Not the sex part. She had plenty of ideas on that. But the day-to-day life of loving another person. Or in this case, persons. Her brain felt like it was on the verge of melting down or imploding. That sounded melodramatic, but she was reeling from their words and that kiss…

Despite all the confused emotions spinning in her mind, she still wanted that perfect night she'd been thinking about minutes ago. That hadn't changed one bit.

"I know it's a lot to take in," Dalton said. "But that's what we were talking about in the kitchen. Talking about how both our wolves see you as our mate. And what to do about it."

Cole held up a hand, looking at her tenderly. "Seems like words are getting in the way. Usually, I prefer to let my actions speak for me. But I want you to know, I kissed you because I wanted to. Simple as that. And now I want more, if you want the same."

Dalton moved in close to her. His voice was almost a whisper. "Let us make this a perfect night for you, Cindy."

He was looking into her eyes, standing very close to her. Her breathing quickened, her need sparked back to life at his words, at his proximity, at his stare. How could she deny it? Her body wanted him. And she wanted Cole, especially after the kiss that had left her knees weak and her senses reeling.

She glanced at Dalton's lips as he slowly leaned toward her. He was going to kiss her. He was giving her the chance to turn away before their lips met. Giving her the chance to tell him no.

But there was no way she would tell him no. She realized how much she wanted this, so she shoved aside any doubts or fears and gave in to her desire. Hadn't she been telling herself that the night seemed magical, as if luck or fate had brought them together? So why not give herself over to it completely? There would never be another night like tonight. She might not believe in the whole mates thing, at least not completely, but that didn't mean she couldn't give in and do something wild. Something she wanted.

Something she *needed*.

Dalton kissed her. Softly at first, and as she yielded to him, he deepened the kiss. His arms came around her, pulling her tightly against his body. She could feel the hard press of his cock against her abdomen. The evidence of his desire only stoked her fires even higher. She was already slick with need, and the more he kissed her, the more aroused she grew.

Cole moved up behind her, brushing aside her hair and kissing her neck, sending a delightful shiver through her body. His hands caressed their way up her sides to finally cup her breasts, drawing a moan from her lips. They took the sound of her pleasure as the encouragement she meant it to be. Dalton's tongue invaded her mouth, and he ran his hands up her thighs to grasp her butt cheeks.

She reached out with trembling fingers and began to undress Dalton, pulling at his clothes, wanting him naked. She knew where this was going, and she wanted to get rid of these annoying barriers of cloth between the three of them.

He ended the kiss and caught her hands.

"Let us do the work," he said in a low voice, deep with promise. "You just enjoy this."

"That's right," Cole murmured against the skin of her neck. "Let us make this special for you. That's all we want."

What could she say to that except yes? Having two men focused on her pleasure? It was like some kind of erotic fantasy springing to life.

Both men began to undress her slowly, baring her skin and covering it with kisses. Piece by piece, her chauffeur uniform came off until she was down to bra and panties.

When Cole reached for her bra hooks, she caught

his hand playfully. "Now you two."

"Our pleasure," Cole said, grinning.

He sauntered to Dalton and pulled him into a kiss. She watched them kiss, their tongues playing against each other. God, it was hot seeing them kiss like that. She was biting her lip to keep in a desperate groan.

Then she stared, practically drooling, as they began to undress each other, yanking off clothes and tossing them aside as if they were in the way. She sucked in a breath when Dalton dropped Cole's pants. Cole's hard cock tented his boxer shorts, and it looked like he had good-sized equipment hidden in there.

A moment later, she got to judge for herself as Dalton slid down Cole's boxers, freeing his cock. It was long and thick, with a dusky head, the slit wet with precum.

Then Cole did the same to Dalton, letting his ski pants fall and pulling down Dalton's boxer shorts. He fondled Dalton's erection, teasing his fingers along the other man's length until he earned a grunt of pleasure from the alpha.

Cole glanced her way, grinning as he stroked Dalton's cock. "Good enough?"

"Better than good," she replied in a husky voice.

Both beautifully naked men moved back to her,

their hot gazes searing along her body. They quickly finished undressing her, removing her bra and letting her large breasts free, then peeling down her panties. It felt wonderful to be naked with them, seeing their desire for her, for each other.

Dalton began to kiss her again, claiming her lips for his own. Cole left them. She was aware of him moving away, already mourning the lost touch of his hands on her body. Dalton shifted his kisses to her neck as he massaged her breasts. As Dalton kissed down to the hollow at the base of her neck, Cindy saw Cole return to them. He was carrying two condoms and a bottle of lube. The sight of the lube made the muscles in her groin flutter and tighten.

She was doing this. She was really going to do this. And she knew it was going to be incredible.

Cole moved up behind her again, drawing a hand up her thigh, nudging her legs apart so that he could trace his fingers along the outside of her slick sex. She felt the tightening need and building pressure deep inside her, a heat that was growing with every passing second.

"Feels like you're ready for us," Cole said, his stare hot and intense.

"No," Dalton said in a rough voice. "Not yet." He leaned in close to her neck, speaking low and fiercely just millimeters from her smoldering skin. "I want her turned-on even more. I want her needing it desperately."

Her body almost shuddered with the desire flooding her, but she gritted her teeth and managed to keep her voice steady as she replied. *Almost* steady. "Y-you think you can do that?"

His laughter was deep and arrogant and utterly delicious. "I know we can." He threw a look at Cole. "Shall we?"

"I'd love to."

She watched in anticipation as Cole stretched out on the couch. His long body with all its tight muscles took up the whole thing, and the couch wasn't small. His cock jutted up from his body, standing from a dark patch of pubic hair. He met her eyes, fisted his cock, and pumped himself several times just for her benefit. Her knees felt a little wobbly.

Grinning, Dalton climbed on the couch too, but opposite Cole, and she realized with a near-swooning surge of lust that they were going to sixty-nine each other. And wasn't that one of the hottest fucking things she'd ever seen in her life?

It was. She had to steady herself against the easy chair as she watched Dalton grip the base of Cole's cock and plunge his mouth down on it. Cole took Dalton's length into his mouth too, working the other man's cock with slow, deliberate strokes. As she watched, he reached up and gripped Dalton's ass cheek hard with his free hand, then began to stroke and tease Dalton's balls and his rear hole.

Cindy couldn't help herself. She needed to take the edge off this building pressure inside her. Reaching down between her thighs, she slid her finger inside her pussy, curling it along her channel. Then she drew her finger along her slit, coaxing her juices over her clit. Her back arched, and her muscles tightened as waves of pleasure and need washed through her. She barely blinked, not wanting to miss an instant of the scene before her. Watching both men pleasuring each other was like an erotic fantasy come to life.

Time seemed to slow. She didn't think, lost in the moment, caught up in seeing their passion for each other. Finally, Dalton pulled his mouth off Cole's cock and growled. "All right, you bastard, if you keep that up, I'm going to shoot off before I'm ready."

Cole drew his lips off Dalton's cock and gave the tip one last lick. He grinned and looked at Cindy. His eyes widened with raw lust when he saw her there with her legs spread wide as she stroked her pussy.

Dalton got off the couch and moved toward her.

His grin was almost arrogant. "Now I think our little mate is ready," he said to Cole.

He drew her to him, fisted a hand in her hair and ravaged her mouth with a kiss that had her head spinning. When he ended the kiss, he guided her to the couch. She could feel the waves of heat from the burning fire. That heat felt divine on her naked skin.

Cole stayed on the couch, his hard cock jutting against his flat, muscular stomach. The tip of his cock glistened with precum and Dalton's saliva. When he moved, his cock left a wet mark along his skin that she had the sudden and intense desire to lick off his stomach. She let her gaze move eagerly over his body, from his blue eyes down his broad chest, to that washboard stomach and beautiful cock, and how his quads bunched when he shifted, readying for her to straddle him.

He reached out and took her hand. Then he drew her closer to him. She went willingly, excitement tingling through her entire body. She felt like she was on fire from the inside, her need so strong she was trembling. The heat from the hearth kept her warm even though she was naked, but even without it, she knew she would feel like she was burning up.

She swung her leg over Cole's body, straddling him. She reached between her spread legs and took his cock in hand. A groan escaped her lips at how hot and silken his skin felt. She ran her thumb over the tip of his cock, sliding over the wetness there as she grinned down at him. He was gritting his teeth, his stare intense as he looked at her naked body. His eyes lingered on her breasts, then dropped lower to where she began to slowly stroke him, and then jumped back up to lock with her gaze. A thrill shot through her at the passion she saw flaring in his eyes.

He wanted her. Badly. As badly as she wanted him.

Dalton's hands settled on her ass, caressing her. She leaned forward a little, and Cole's hands found her breasts. He began to fondle her breasts, tracing his thumbs over her hard nipples. His touch sent mini jolts of pleasure through her body, making her pussy even wetter.

Behind her, Dalton's hands left her ass. She heard him tear open one of the condoms and toss the wrapper aside. Then he stroked his fingers through her pubic hair, trailing over her hot lower lips before he began to unroll the condom over Cole's cock.

She waited impatiently, her core throbbing with the need to be filled.

Dalton chuckled. "Just wait, sweetheart. Let me

prepare you right."

"Hurry," she whispered, desperate to sink down on Cole's dick and have him fill her. She wanted them both inside her. She wanted to come, to reach that shuddering completeness.

Cole's hands distracted her, sliding along her sides and back up to cup her breasts. He gently pinched and twisted her erect nipples, not enough to hurt, but the friction was delicious.

Behind her, Dalton sheathed himself, then poured lube into his hand. His coated fingers began to tease along her pussy lips, but when he found how wet she was, he moved to her other hole. He delicately traced his finger around her hole, and the sensation had her breathing ragged.

She cried out when he worked the lube inside her, teasing that muscle until it clenched tighter then gradually yielded to his pressure. Carefully, he worked the lube inside her, slipping another finger inside her and scissoring ever so slightly to open her for him.

When he was done, he gently withdrew his fingers and gave her a playful smack on the ass. She yelped in surprise and laughed.

Dalton grinned at her. "Damn, I need that ass of yours, beautiful. Now sink down on Cole and lean forward."

She reached between her legs and grabbed Cole's hard cock. She lined it up with her pussy and slowly eased down on him. Her slick walls stretched to take him deep. A shuddering sigh escaped her lips as she leaned forward, lying along Cole's body. His hands cradled her head as he turned her lips to his and kissed her deeply.

Leaning forward gave Dalton the angle he needed to her back entrance while she pressed herself against Cole's amazing body and let him dominate her lips. Her legs were spread wide, and Dalton straddled Cole, maneuvering behind her and resting his hands on her wide hips. His cockhead nudged at her rear hole, teasing her, then letting her relax a little. She was already distracted by Cole though, who was thrusting upward into her pussy in a steady rhythm.

She let out a sigh as Dalton pushed inside her. Even with the lube, there was a brief moment of discomfort and burning, but Dalton held her steady and eased his way in carefully until he was fully seated inside her.

Then they both began to fuck her.

Waves of pleasure soon fogged her brain. Her eyes rolled back, and she made little helpless, needy moans of bliss. The sensation of being filled with two cocks was mind-blowing. It was almost too much to take. She couldn't move because they were setting the rhythm, building speed, Cole thrusting up into her and Dalton gripping her hips tightly as he pounded forward deep inside her.

At first, she'd wanted to come so badly it was like a fever inside her. But when she felt that orgasm building fast, she suddenly wanted to hold it off for as long as possible. She wanted this moment to last, this incredible connection between the three of them. Her thoughts were half-formed, hazy with the pleasure rushing through her. She felt as if she couldn't take this, two men driving into her at once, stretching her, filling her. They seemed to own every part of her body, claiming everything, especially below the waist, one cock thrusting into her pussy, the other sinking deep into her ass, and with every thrust, his ball sack slapping lightly against her perineum.

She didn't move. She let them set their rhythm, their pace. She lay along Cole's body, her breasts pressing against his chest. He kissed her deeply, then sent trails of kisses along her neck and up to her ear. The kisses didn't set off the same fireworks as the intense pulses of pleasure from down below—those sensations were too overwhelming—but they did drive her ever closer to the edge. They made her feel like her whole body and all her bliss were being commanded by these men, that they were driving her to the brink of ecstasy and she never wanted it to stop.

She wasn't going to last much longer. It was too much. Too good. Suddenly, she shattered around them with a sharp cry of pleasure. Her muscles went rigid, pulsing as her orgasm shuddered through her. She came so hard she could barely breathe.

Cole kissed her fiercely, claiming her lips as if drinking in the sound of her pleasure, her moans and cries. Behind her, she heard Dalton growl, a low, almost feral sound of his building orgasm. Both of them began to fuck her faster and harder, trying to catch up with her now that she'd come.

"So fucking tight," Dalton groaned.

His words and the desperate edge to his voice sent another thrill racing through her.

The sound of flesh slapping flesh was loud and constant. Her thoughts were barely coherent with the pleasure still surging through her, the waves of her orgasm gradually diminishing, but her body still feeling delightful bliss from coming so hard.

Below her, Cole tensed and groaned, his release taking him. He pumped into her faster, riding out his orgasm to the last. She felt his cock pulsing inside her. Finally, he slowed his thrusts and dragged her into another soul-deep kiss.

Dalton's fingers tightened where he gripped her hips as he plowed her, rocking her forward with every thrust. She knew he wouldn't last long.

He sucked in a shuddering breath when he finally hit the place of no return, grabbing her ass cheeks tightly as he drove one last time, all the way in her, and his cock began to pulse as he shot his hot cum.

His breathing was quick and ragged. She knew from the sound that he'd had a good time. That all three of them had enjoyed themselves beyond words. She could barely move. Her bones felt like jelly, and her mind was fuzzy with pleasure.

Carefully, Dalton gripped the base of the condom and withdrew from her. Cole was still in her, but his cock was softening after he'd come. She missed the feeling of them both inside her. It had been an incredible sensation of connection. The fact that it was between three people made it all the more special and rare. Something she would never forget for as long as she lived.

Dalton headed to the bathroom to clean up. She nuzzled Cole's neck, lying bonelessly draped along the length of his body. He held her tightly, one hand slowly stroking her hair.

"That was the most amazing thing ever," Cole said softly.

"I know," she purred. "I don't think I've ever come that hard before." She nipped at his neck, then licked the spot. "I think it makes up for being kidnapped."

He laughed, the deep rumble in his chest shaking her a little. Dalton returned and kissed his way up her spine.

"Let's get her to bed," Dalton said to Cole.

"I'm just going to sleep right here," Cindy muttered. "It's nice and so warm."

"Dalton can't exactly sleep on top of us on the couch." Cole shifted a little, pulling his cock out of her. "And we can't make him sleep on the floor."

"I refuse to move." She nuzzled deeper against him, feeling completely relaxed and good.

Gently, Dalton slipped his arms under her and effortlessly lifted her into his arms. He held her as if she were a bride he intended to carry across the threshold. She wrapped her arms around the back of his neck, snuggling against his naked chest. She was all about the snuggles right now.

"Come on, beautiful. It'll be more comfortable in

the bedroom."

"If you insist," she murmured. "And if you carry me there…"

"Our princess wants to be carried," Dalton said to Cole, sounding amused.

"The last time I tried that, she hit me over the head," Cole shot back. "So be careful."

She had the feeling they were never going to let her live that down. "That was all a complete misunderstanding."

A naked Cole led the way as Dalton carried her, giggling, into the bedroom. Cole pulled back the sheets on the bed, then stepped into the bathroom to dispose of the condom. Dalton got into bed beside her, giving her a long, lingering kiss. It wasn't passionate so much as very tender and caring. Soon Cole was back, climbing into bed with them.

Cindy curled up between them. Their naked bodies were so warm. She barely needed the sheet, much less the comforter, even with the snowy night outside. It was so nice and toasty lying there between them.

She was calm, sated. She had zero regrets. Her body certainly held no misgivings. After that earth-shaking orgasm, she was feeling happy and satisfied. Her limbs felt like cooked noodles. Her lips were still tingling from the kisses.

The three of them didn't speak. There was nothing that needed to be said. Cole fell asleep first. She could tell from the change in the sound of his breathing. He lay next to her with an arm thrown across her body. Then Dalton drifted off. His body was pressed up against hers, practically spooning her. She loved the silken feel of his skin against hers. And, of course, his body heat.

But she didn't fall asleep. Her brain was too excited even if her body was exhausted. She simply lay there, looking out the bedroom window at the falling snow. It was so peaceful and perfect. Tranquil.

She knew that wouldn't last. Tomorrow she'd have to deal with the limo and getting herself back home. But right now, she didn't want the night to end. That's why she couldn't sleep. If she slept, this incredible dream would be over...

Eventually though, she did slip off to sleep, and she didn't wake until the sun came up.

CHAPTER EIGHT

Dalton

Dalton woke up to bright sunlight streaming through the window and pooling on the wood floor like melted butter. He stretched and sat up. He was naked, and his body felt great. His wolf was sated and quiet, content, and that had his spirit at ease. He glanced around, hoping to see a naked Cindy and a naked Cole lying in bed beside him.

The bed was disappointingly empty. Then he heard Cindy's light, happy laugh coming from deeper in Cole's house. The sound of her laughter immediately lifted his heart, surprising him with the warmth that swept through him. Was this what it was like with true mates? This feeling of warmth and completeness?

Maybe it was, maybe it wasn't, but he could definitely get used to it.

Next, he heard Cole's deep voice, but with the bedroom door closed, he couldn't make out the words. It was clear they were both happy and chatting with each other. He rolled out of bed, already grinning. He was eager to be with them again. His wolf was even more excited.

His brain was already in planning mode. First thing was to get some food in his belly. After that, he would help Cindy sort out any problems over the limo crash. From the look of the bright blue sky beyond the trees, today was going to be sunny, even if it was still cold. The plows would be out in force. Life would be getting back to normal.

Well, normal for everyone else. Because Dalton's new normal had to include his two mates. Last night had sealed it for him. He needed these two in his life.

He pulled on his pants and walked out of the room barefoot and bare-chested. His shifter body temp always ran hot, but with the heat running, the house was nice and toasty, even out of the bedcovers. After a stop in the bathroom, he padded down the hall to the kitchen.

His mouth was already watering over the aromas of bacon, eggs, toast, and orange juice he could smell wafting from the kitchen. His stomach growled with more ferocity than an angry wolf.

Cole was at the stove, cooking away. He was wearing jeans and a flannel shirt, his hair still wet from a shower. Dalton felt a pulse of lust at the sight of Cole's broad, muscular back as he bent over the skillets.

Cindy leaned against the counter, standing in almost the same place that Dalton had stood last night when he'd been warning Cole that she belonged to him. She looked absolutely stunning, also wearing a flannel shirt that had to belong to Cole. The shirt hem came down to mid-thigh, and she wasn't wearing pants, so he could admire those curvy legs of hers.

Cindy gave him the sweetest smile he'd ever seen. "Hi, sexy. You're even cuter first thing in the morning."

He snorted and rubbed a hand through his bed-head hair. "Yeah, the real picture of style, I'm sure."

"The lady doesn't lie," Cole said with that cocky tilt to his lips. "So the question is, are you hungry?"

"I'm starving. Smells great."

A few minutes later, he had a plate of hot food in his hands and was shoveling down breakfast as fast as he could get it in his mouth. Cindy and Cole were standing with him in the kitchen, eating, drinking coffee, and chatting.

It felt a little odd to be standing around a kitchen and downing breakfast with two other people, but it also felt exactly right too. To him, it felt like they'd always known each other. Even the friction between him and Cole had morphed into something easy and smooth. Now it felt more like the good-natured teasing between packmates.

He liked this feeling of closeness and warmth. He had it when he was with his pack, but this was even more intense, and he seemed to feel it in a deeper, richer way. The laughter came easy and often. After sharing Cindy, even his human side didn't feel jealous of Cole. Dalton would much rather kiss the man than brawl with him.

Following breakfast, they dressed and got ready to head back to town. Dalton helped Cole shovel snow. They used his snow blower to dig out Cole's truck, which had a plow on the front. Then he rode with Cole as they plowed the rest of the drive to the main road.

"Looks like we're in business," Cole said when they discovered the main road had been plowed.

Dalton only nodded. Now that they had a way back to civilization, he found himself reluctant to leave.

Last night, Cindy had talked about their time together seeming magical, like something fated. Now he didn't want it to end.

They picked up Cindy from the house and soon were on the road back to town. They followed the two-lane road through the trees and lower slopes as it wound its way down to the plain. Even plowed, the road was treacherous. Going was slow.

Cindy had her cell phone in her hand. As soon as she got a good signal, she called Mirage. She explained what had happened and that she was on the way back.

Dalton could hear the woman on the other end of the line reply, "Thank God you're all right, sweetie. We were all so worried. We called the sheriffs when you didn't come back, but the roads were too dangerous until they were plowed. This storm has caused ten kinds of havoc."

"Thanks, Amanda," Cindy said. "A friend is giving me a ride back to Mirage. I'll explain everything and do the paperwork when I get there."

"And then we're going out for drinks, and you can tell me all the juicy details. Oh, I'm so happy to hear your voice. You have no idea."

Cindy said goodbye and disconnected. She was smiling from ear to ear. Her friend Amanda's concern had clearly touched her.

Conversation was muted for the rest of the ride. It wasn't awkward, but none of them seemed to be looking forward to leaving each other. Dalton assumed Cole would take them to the nearest small town, but Cole told them he was driving them all the way back to Boulder. Cindy asked to be taken to the Mirage Confidential offices. Dalton wanted her to be dropped off first, in case there was some issue with her boss over the accident. He wouldn't stand idly by if this was going to cost her the job. He had wealth, and he had influence. He'd happily use both to make sure she was shielded from any repercussions. After all, she'd been out there in the storm because of him.

It was after one in the afternoon when they finally reached the Mirage offices and garages in Boulder. Cole parked the truck, but as soon as Dalton helped Cindy down, a woman charged out of the office doors. Her sudden appearance was surprising—almost alarming. It reminded him of last night when Cindy burst out of Cole's front door in the middle of the blizzard and nearly ran him down.

The woman practically knocked Cindy over with her hug. "It's so good to see you! I was so worried. You don't even know!"

Cindy looked a bit overwhelmed by her friend's reaction. "Thanks, Amanda. It's good to be back. Did you tell the boss that the limo's still back in the mountains, wrapped around a tree?"

Amanda had shiny, dark hair and big brown eyes. She wore a fashionable leather jacket and huge earrings. He put her age somewhere in the early thirties range. She was human, not a shifter, but her scent told him she was kind and caring.

"He knows," she replied, waving her hands as if to dismiss Cindy's worries. "He just needs a few details so we can send out a tow truck. He was more worried about you. We're all glad that you're safe." She eyed Cindy critically. "I don't see any gaping wounds. Any internal injuries?"

"Nope," Cindy replied. "Some good Samaritans helped me out. This is Cole, and this is Dalton."

Amanda's dark, thick eyebrows rose high on her forehead. "Our client?"

Cindy's eyes widened. "Um. Yes. I meant to say 'Mr. Kincaid.'"

Dalton put on his winningest smile. "Please call me Dalton. I don't like to stand on ceremony." He put his hand on Cole's shoulder and gave him a reassuring squeeze. "To be honest, both of us owe a debt of gratitude to Cole here. Not only did he give us a ride, he let us crash overnight at his cabin to ride out the storm."

Amanda beamed at them. "Glad to hear country hospitality isn't dead in this day and age. Everyone at Mirage thanks you both for taking care of our girl here. She's quite special to us."

"I reckon she's special to quite a few people," Cole said kindly. "Including us, now. But I was happy to help. These days, we all have to remember how important it is to care for one another."

Cindy looked at Cole, then at Dalton. Her eyes were a little watery, as if she was fighting back tears. Her voice hitched a little with emotion when she said, "I...I better get inside and get this paperwork settled and talk to the boss..."

"Are you going to be okay?" Dalton said, taking her hand and squeezing it. His protective instincts were rearing up now. He didn't want to be pushy, but he did want to make certain things would be fine between her and Mirage.

She smiled warmly at him. "I am. Thanks to you and Cole."

He wanted to kiss her, but he could sense that she wasn't ready for that level of public display of affection yet.

He wasn't offended. They would get there. This sure as hell wouldn't be the last time he'd see her or Cole.

He took out his smartphone. "Give me your number. I'll call you later tonight."

She paused, her expression suddenly uncertain. He felt a flash of unease, especially at her scent. Her scent was that of a person in conflict, someone of two minds about a thing and facing a tough decision. He didn't understand what was wrong. He wanted her number. He hadn't asked for her hand in marriage.

Not yet anyway.

He could see it in her eyes when she reached a decision…although his nose was still telling him she remained uncertain and conflicted about it.

"Okay," she said, pulling out her phone to read off her number. "Are you ready?"

He reached for his cell phone…and realized he'd lost it last night in the small avalanche that had sent him tumbling down from the road. He frowned and rubbed a hand across his face. "I forgot. I lost my phone last night."

"That's okay. Give me your number, and I'll put it in my phone."

Now wasn't this an embarrassing moment? He'd never memorized his cell phone number. It was a new phone, less than a year old, and he'd never bothered to learn it. It was stored in the phone after all, easy to access…or had been easy until he'd lost it. On top of that, he didn't have any business cards on hand. He didn't even have his wallet. After all, he'd been skiing, and he'd expected to be driven home by a limo.

"Yeah, about that," he said a bit sheepishly. "New phone. Hadn't memorized the number yet." He glanced at Cole. "Did you bring your phone?"

Cole shrugged. "I don't own a cell phone. No reception out where I'm at, remember? I like being off the grid."

Amanda shook her head and broke in. "These times we live in." She reached into the breast pocket of her jacket and pulled out a pen and a slip of paper. She handed it to Cindy so she could write down her cell phone number.

Cindy scrawled down numbers, writing fast. She handed the paper to Dalton, but for some reason, she glanced away and didn't look him in the eyes.

Cole put a hand on her shoulder. "You want us to stick around? Help with the paperwork? Believe it or not, I can write my full name. I know Dalton's probably impressed by that."

She giggled, her face suddenly brightening.

Instead of feeling a surge of jealousy, Dalton was deeply grateful his male mate could make her laugh so easily. The lack of jealousy was even more evidence that things had truly and deeply changed between the three of them.

"No," Cindy replied. "I'll take care of everything from here. But thank you." She hesitated again, looking at both of them in turn. A tear ran down her cheek, and she quickly wiped it away. "I really mean it. I'll never forget…"

She stopped, choked up. Another flash of concern went through him. He understood that some people were emotional, but it wasn't as if she would never see them again. He didn't know why her scent was so confusing to him now. Maybe it was just a reaction to everything that had happened, the accident, the storm, their time together. It was a lot to pack into one night.

He gave her a gentle, reassuring smile. "Don't worry. Everything's going to be fine."

But she didn't say anything. She only nodded, hesitated again, and then began to walk toward the front door of the modern-looking office building.

Amanda moved to follow her, but Dalton pulled her aside.

"I'd like a moment, if I may," he told her quickly.

"I want to pay the bonus I promised. Make sure I'm charged for it."

Her eyebrows rose again. "You sure? I mean, the wreck is on our shoulders. I know you were put out. We apologize for any inconvenience and would be happy to reimburse you."

He grinned. "Good customer service, but yes, it was on me. She was out there to pick me up. I was the one who thought we could beat the storm. So I don't need any reimbursement or apologies."

"That storm surprised even the weather people. But I know she'll appreciate your kind gesture." She gave him a measuring look. "Thank you. Not everyone would do the same."

He nodded. He would've happily given Cindy a far higher bonus, but he was afraid it might go over wrong. Especially if he wasn't there to tell her about it in person. He didn't want to offend her by throwing money around. Money was a sensitive subject for people. He sure as hell didn't want her thinking he was paying her off like she was some kind of escort he'd bought for the night. He didn't want to take that chance.

No, he'd have plenty of time to spoil both his mates rotten later. It made him happy to use his wealth to help people. He funded multiple charities, paid for healthcare and college educations for members of his pack, donated to good causes and to help those in need after natural disasters. Even though his mates might need his love more than his money, he was more than happy to share. He knew that sharing with them would make *him* happy.

Amanda assured him she'd take care of the bonus and keep an eye on Cindy. She said goodbye to Cole and headed back inside the building where Cindy had gone.

They both watched her leave. The woman seemed to know something was up between the three of them. Dalton didn't care if she found out the truth or not, but he also intended to let Cindy set the pace. He wanted her comfortable with their threesome relationship. That was why he hadn't insisted on the goodbye kiss he'd wanted. He was content to follow her lead and respect her wishes until she was ready to take their relationship to the next level.

"Miss her already, don't you?" Cole asked him quietly.

"I do."

"Same here." Cole met his eyes and slapped a hand down on his shoulder. "Now, where can I take you?"

* * *

Cole

After leaving the Mirage offices, Cole took Dalton back to his sprawling mansion north of Boulder. The house was probably ten times as big as Cole's cabin, with a million-dollar view of the distant mountains. The mansion was one of those modern "country" ones with lots of glass, lots of wood, a fancy barn, a carriage house, sprawling decks and all that. Five-car detached garage. Fountains. Huge windows. He guessed it had to be at least four thousand square feet or more.

He tried not to be impressed, but he was anyway. He loved where he lived, right in the mountains, nestled in the trees, with only the distant sound of occasional traffic on the mountain road to remind him there were other people around. But this place sure was fancy. Cindy would love it.

He gritted his teeth. Yeah, she would love it. Who wouldn't? Why would she like his little place when she could have something like this?

He was clearly on edge. Ever since he'd dropped Cindy off, something had been bothering him *and* his wolf. Cindy had been happy...and then she hadn't been happy, right when they'd reached Mirage.

Was it because the three of them were splitting up, going their separate ways for now? Or was something else bothering her? If her coworker hadn't been there with them, he would've pressed her to share her feelings. Women loved sharing their feelings, didn't they? Seemed like a necessary time for it. But the coworker's presence complicated things. It stopped them from having the kind of goodbye Cindy deserved. So the whole thing had left him unsettled and out of sorts.

Dalton opened the door and jumped down from the truck after Cole stopped in front of the big mansion. Cole did the same, stretching his muscles to work out the kinks of the long ride. He'd spent more time behind the wheel today than he had in months. Usually, he only used the truck to head to town for supplies every week and that was it.

"Nice place," Cole said, putting his hands on his hips as he stared at Dalton's mansion.

The other alpha glanced at him. "You want to come in?"

"I do, but I should be heading back. There's more snow expected later tonight. I don't want to get caught out here in the city if there's another storm."

"Fair enough. I need to touch base with my pack

too."

They stood there together, looking at the big house, neither of them talking.

Finally, Dalton broke the silence. "So what happens now?"

Cole shrugged. "Don't know."

"You're welcome in my pack."

"I'm not much of a pack type." He paused, deciding that sounded ungrateful for the offer. "But thank you."

"I know."

More silence. Not uncomfortable but still weighty.

He felt a deep connection to Dalton, one far deeper than their time together could explain. It was the wolf side of them that forged a deep, near instantaneous bond. It was why he'd reacted so strongly to Cindy when he'd dated women before, shifters and humans alike, without the same deep connection so soon after meeting.

"This is going to work," Dalton told him, rubbing his chin in thought. He hadn't shaved, so his fingers rasped over his stubble.

Cole like seeing him a little rumpled, a little roughed up. It made him seem down to earth. Approachable. Lovable. Instead of the imperious alpha that so many pack leaders wasted so much time portraying. Another reason Cole didn't bother with packs. He was glad Dalton believed this...whatever the three of them had together would work.

Cole wasn't so sure, but he kept his voice carefully neutral. "You think so?"

Dalton's eyes narrowed as if he could sense Cole's uncertainty.

"I know it," he said. "Why? You having doubts?"

Cole shook his head, rocking back on this boot heels as he thought about it. "Cindy's not from our world. She's a hardworking sweetheart of a gal, but she's not a shifter. I'm a lone wolf, living off the grid. You're an alpha with a pack to lead."

"So what? I don't allow racist wolves in my pack. If they have a problem with humans, they either change their opinion or they get out."

"She's going to feel like an outsider. Same as I would."

Now Dalton's eyes flashed with anger. "What are you saying? That I'm the one making you both feel that way?"

"No, not on purpose." He took a deep breath, trying to gather his thoughts. "I know what our wolves want. But I'm not sure it's going to be easy."

Cole wasn't from Dalton's wealthy, high-society

world. He'd inherited his land and the house from his father. Cole's career had been busting his ass in the Marines, and nobody ever got rich there. He wasn't going to fool himself into claiming he was anywhere close to Dalton's league. True, Cole was better looking, stronger, and his dick was a good inch longer, but all that aside, Dalton was still rich as hell, and nothing was gonna change that.

"Look," Dalton said. "I'll solve this. I'll get us all together. Book an entire Caribbean cruise ship just for the three of us and the pack, so you both can get to know them like I know them."

Cole shook his head. "That's damn generous, but you still don't get it. I doubt Cindy can miss that much work. She has bills to pay. And I'm not sure my wolf can handle being stuck on a boat with a bunch of wolves subservient to you." He pointed back toward the mountains. "I need to run. It keeps me centered."

"They aren't subservient and you know it, Cole," Dalton growled. "So don't be giving me your lone-wolf bullshit. And it's not a 'boat,' it's a freaking cruise ship, for God's sake!"

Cole didn't say anything. He didn't have anything to say. It was endearing that Dalton was so good-hearted and generous, but he was still as naïve as only a wealthy person who had everything he'd ever wanted could be.

Dalton eyed him. "You don't have anything to say to that?"

"Hey, I hope I'm wrong. I've got her number. You've got her number. I intend to call, even if I have to use the last payphone in Boulder."

"You sound like you're giving up."

"Not even close."

But was he? No, when he thought about it, no. Still, there were some things he couldn't deny. Even if the three of them were meant to be together, life didn't always have a happy ending for everyone. He'd learned that lesson long ago as a Marine. Cole hadn't been particularly lucky in love either.

Maybe that had changed.

Maybe it hadn't.

He could see Dalton was intent on proving him wrong…and he loved the other man for it.

Instead of arguing the point, he pulled Dalton close. Both his hands clenched in the man's coat. He leaned in and kissed Dalton. He poured everything he had into the kiss.

When he finally drew back, they were both breathing hard.

Dalton's lips curled into a small smile. "Is that my

goodbye kiss?"

"Yeah, it is, you smug bastard. So I hope you enjoyed it."

The smile widened. "I did."

Dalton made his way to his front door. Cole walked back to his truck and got inside. He didn't drive off until Dalton opened his door and turned back to wave. Cole raised a hand in return. Then he started the truck and started down the long driveway and out the fancy gate.

He turned on the radio because it was too damn quiet without Cindy and Dalton here with him. He set out for home.

He'd woken up so happy this morning, but now… Now he couldn't deny that his heart sat heavy in his chest. It was strange because he had no reason to feel down. No logical reason whatsoever.

But driving away, he couldn't escape the feeling that he was leaving them both behind and wouldn't see them again…

CHAPTER NINE

Cindy

One week later…

Cindy marked off the last item on her checklist as she restocked her limo for tonight's assignment. This was a different limousine of course. The one that had gone over the side of the mountain was in the body shop being repaired. It was part of her job to make sure the bar and everything else in the back of the limo was restocked before she left. She tried to focus on the simple, straightforward tasks in front of her.

She tried not to feel the empty hole in her chest

where her heart had been.

It had been a week since she'd last seen Cole and Dalton. Her cell phone had been silent. Of course it had. Because she'd given both of them a wrong number. The last digit had been wrong.

And she'd done it on purpose, thinking it was the right thing. She knew everyone on the planet would think her crazy for doing it. But she'd been afraid. Afraid they wouldn't call. Afraid that it was nothing more than a wild, one-night stand for them, and that would shatter her heart completely.

So instead, she'd sabotaged everything and simply cut her own heart out so they couldn't do it first.

They hadn't called her. She didn't have their numbers, so she hadn't called them.

It was over.

She missed both her werewolves deeply. The whole week had been hell. She'd been crying. Sleeping all the time. Dragging herself into work looking half dead. Listening to Amanda lecture her and fret over her and shake her head and fret some more. She'd hung out with her girlfriends, Rachel and Deb, though she didn't tell them the details no matter how much they'd pried. She'd only told them that it was man trouble.

It was only partly the truth. Because it was man

trouble that she'd started. *She'd* chosen to end things after one perfect night because she hadn't wanted her heart broken.

But she'd made the right choice, hadn't she?

With every passing day, she began to suspect more and more that she'd made a terrible choice. Self-doubt had crept in, tormenting her. Especially at night when she couldn't sleep.

No, she *had* done the right thing. That whole business about her being their mate was just talk. They had just been using her because she was warm and more than willing. After scratching their itches, Dalton had moved back to his werewolf pack and his businesses and charities, and Cole had gone back to being a lone-wolf mountain man. Or that's what she assumed anyway.

Like she'd said, it was for the best. She wasn't the kind of girl a man like Dalton brought home to mother. She didn't wear the right clothes. She hadn't gone to the right schools. She didn't know the right people…or come from the right people.

And Cole was too disconnected from everyone. Cole wanted to live in the woods and be a wolf. If she had to leave her friends, family, and grocery stores behind for the wilderness, it would eventually drive her bonkers.

Okay, it had been a bit of a test too. Yes, it was a bit underhanded, but she wanted to see if either man would track her down again if they ran up against an obstacle like having the wrong phone number. That would tell her if they'd only enjoyed her company the night of the blizzard but all that talk of mates and love had only been to get her panties off.

It was fine. She was a big girl. She hadn't seen them in a week, so she had her answer, didn't she? That was best. She didn't belong with shifters anyway. What was it her grandpa had always said? Like with like.

On the other hand, her grandpa had always been a racist, bigoted asshole who made Thanksgiving dinner hell, so why would she ever listen to his stupid advice?

She finished checking all the champagne flutes and brandy snifters, making sure they were clean and secure before she began driving. Everything looked good, fully stocked and cleaned. She signed off on her inspection report on her computer tablet.

Cindy was locking up the limo again when Amanda poked her head into the garage area.

"Sweetie, you have a visitor!" Amanda gushed, a bright smile on her face.

She froze. Her heart began to beat faster. She swallowed, and her throat made a weird clicking-gulping noise that didn't sound human. Could it be…?

"Who is it?" she finally managed to say, but Amanda had already vanished again.

Cindy stared at the door, knowing in her heart who had come but not daring to believe it. A second later, her feelings were justified when Dalton walked through the door.

He was wearing a sharp, designer suit that fit him perfectly, a beautiful blue tie, and leather shoes so brilliantly shiny they rivaled the gleam on her washed and waxed limo. He didn't have a hair out of place, and his dark eyes held that mixture of warmth and intensity that sent a thrill tingling straight through her. She'd missed that gaze, that smile. The way he looked at her right before he kissed her…

She quickly pushed those thoughts away. They were dangerous. Especially right now.

Dalton put his hands in his pockets, rocked up on his toes, and smiled at her. "It's good to see you."

"It's good to see you too, Dalton," she replied…and meant every word. "Is…is Cole with you?"

"It's just me." But from the look in his eyes, he wanted Cole here too.

Dalton crossed the garage toward her. He glanced at the limos sitting ready for tonight's clients. Then he looked her over again, and heat flashed in his eyes. "I forgot how tempting you look in that uniform. It brings back some great memories."

Seeing him again brought back a flood of memories for her too. Like the feel of his hands on her body, his lips pressed against hers, how he'd filled her when he'd been inside her...

He stopped in front of her, but he didn't embrace her. His eyes searched hers. Then he pulled a cell phone out of his pocket and held it up.

"I tried calling you. Wrong number. I double-checked it with Cole, and he had the same number. I would've driven here to see you, but unavoidable business matters got in the way. I had to fly to New York for a few days. I came here as soon as I got back to Colorado."

Her chest suddenly felt like it was a sheet of tinfoil being crumpled into a tight ball. Her thoughts were spinning, tossed around by the emotions twisting through her. He hadn't called because she'd given him the wrong number. He hadn't come to see her because he'd been out of town. She felt lightheaded with relief...and deeply contrite too.

She took a deep breath to steady herself. She wasn't going to lie to him. She couldn't. "I gave you the wrong number."

His mouth tightened, and his eyes narrowed. "I don't understand."

She could see the mix of annoyance and hurt in his eyes. She didn't care about the annoyance, but the hurt… That hurt her right back because she knew that *she* was the cause of it.

"I'll tell you exactly why," she said, her voice a little shaky. Though this certainly wasn't the place she would've chosen for this conversation. "Look at you. You're like some handsome, wealthy prince. You lead a pack of people who count on you. You're important. Now look at me. I'm just a girl with too-thick thighs and too big an ass for this uniform who drives rich people around for a living."

"I don't like when you talk about yourself like that," Dalton said, the rumble in his voice just short of a growl. "You're more than any of that. You're beautiful. You—"

"Stop. I'm not fishing for compliments or anything like that. Let's be honest. I don't belong in your social circle. I would never fit in. I don't want to be in that kind of hoity-toity lifestyle either if you want the truth. I'm not the kind of person who can talk about caviar and houses in the Hamptons and dropping twenty-thousand on a designer dress. That's not who I am." She glared at him, putting her hands on her hips. "I know I'm a fool for it. I know I should jump at the chance. But I also know I won't be happy in that life."

"Well, you have one thing down," he said slowly. "You've thrown me for a loop from the moment I first saw you until right this very moment. At least you're consistent."

"I'm sorry, that wasn't all either."

"There's more?"

"I'm not a werewolf."

He rubbed chin, watching her. "So I noticed. But you're as feisty as one."

She didn't know how to take that, so she chose not to respond to it. Instead, she pressed on, barely able to get the words out as more than a whisper. "This is hard for me, Dalton."

Sympathy filled his eyes. He gentled his tone. "I know." He reached out and traced his thumb over her jaw to her lower lip. It was a tender gesture. "I want to kiss you. Every part of me wants it. But I am listening."

She moved back out of reach. She couldn't tell him how much she wanted him to kiss her right now. When he touched her, she doubted everything she'd forced herself to believe since giving him the wrong phone number. When he touched her, he made her believe that this could work. He made her want to risk her heart chasing this crazy dream of happiness.

"I'm not a werewolf," she continued, pushing away her reaction to his touch. "I'm just a human. I won't fit in with your pack. I can't change into a wolf and run with you and Cole. I will always be different. I'll always be an outsider."

"No, Cindy. You're wrong. We're better than that. It's not fair if you don't give us a chance to prove it."

"Even if you... Even if you loved me now, I know that over time, you'd grow apart from me."

It broke her heart to say all of that. Her throat felt so tight and hot that she could barely breathe, much less continue speaking. Her vision blurred with tears. Two fat teardrops spilled from her lashes and ran down her cheeks.

But she managed to keep from breaking down in sobs. There was that at least.

Again, he moved close to her. His hand wiped away those tears. She let him do it. She let him do it because she was greedy and she wanted one last touch, even though it hurt her heart. She'd spent all week believing she'd made a mistake. But now that he was here again, all her reasons for ending things cleanly before…before she could fall in love with Dalton and Cole any more than she already had…all those reasons rushed back into her mind.

He looked down at her, his eyes showing his feelings clearly—his care…his affection. Not love. It couldn't be love.

Could it?

"This isn't over, Cindy," he said, the confidence clear in his tone. "Because it's not simply about you and me. It's about Cole, you, and me. I understand your fears. But that's all they are. Fears. So as your mate, I'm going to prove those fears are empty. I'm going to prove myself to you. You have my word."

If he had gone for the kiss, she would've kissed him back. She wouldn't have been able to help herself. Her heart felt like it was being torn in two different directions. Oh, she badly wanted to believe he was telling the truth. She wanted to believe that she had only been listening to her fears and not her heart. She wanted to believe she had made a mistake.

Without another word, Dalton turned and left the garage. She stood there, staring at the door he'd left through. She wanted him to come back. She wanted Cole here with them. She wanted to drag both of them into the back of one of these limos and make the springs rock. To lose herself in their touches, their kisses.

She wanted…them to love her. She wanted them to prove her wrong.

Hot tears began to run down her cheeks. She leaned against the limo and hid her face in her hands.

After a little while, Amanda came in to check on her. Without a word, she rushed over and drew Cindy into a hug. Because she was a friend, Amanda didn't ask what had happened. She just comforted her.

CHAPTER TEN

Dalton

Right now, Dalton had the kind of focus he only had when fighting another wolf or on the hunt. He knew exactly what he wanted. Cindy and Cole.

He knew what was in danger. Their chance at a future together. Their chance at happiness.

Dalton down-shifted as he put the fancy silver Koenigsegg Trevita around one of the tight curves, then rocked out of the other end of the turn. The snow from the storms had melted, and the road was clear. The sky was a bright, cloudless blue. The day was beautiful, but he didn't pay it any mind except to be grateful that it wasn't snowing or icy out.

He had other things on his mind. He was racing into the mountains, headed to Cole's place. He hadn't seen Cole since the day after the blizzard. That damn board meeting in New York had really screwed him over.

He should've called out and missed the meeting. He should've sent one of his people to handle it.

It had seemed like such a little thing at the time. He owned a lot of companies, and he traveled a lot every year to other cities. The trip to New York had been four days out of his life. Normally, that wasn't a problem. Now it was looking like those had been four crucial days not to miss.

But he hadn't foreseen this. Maybe he could chalk it up to typical male cluelessness, but the fears Cindy confiding in him had seemed to come out of nowhere. At least to his mind, anyway.

Yes, on an intellectual level, he understood where she was coming from...but he was also frustrated. Why was she so eager to find reasons things couldn't work out between the three of them? Why was Dalton the only one who seemed to believe they had a chance?

And where the hell was Cole? Dalton needed him for this. He couldn't convince her that the three of them had a future together without Cole by his side, giving his support.

He steered the sports car out of another tight curve and floored it. The high-performance car screamed down the road. He was driving fast, pushing the car on the challenging roads. Strangely, driving fast soothed him. It took his mind off the panic bubbling just below the surface. He'd done all he could to stay confident and steadfast when she'd been telling him how the three of them had no future together.

His mate, telling him there was no future together.

Like hell. She was wrong. He was going to prove it to her. He was going to show her how much she meant to him. How important she was. That he loved her, because judging by the intensity of his feelings, that was what this was. Love. And that love would only grow and deepen for his two mates over time.

But first, he had to prove that love to Cindy. To do that, he had to find out what the hell Cole was doing. Because without Cole, this was dead in the water.

Soon he spotted Cole's driveway off the main road. He slowed and turned, driving up to the house. He parked right behind Cole's truck and got out. He expected Cole to come outside to greet him. His sports car's high-performance engine was a lot of things, but quiet was not one of them. But there was no sign of Cole. No smoke coming from the chimney either. In fact, the house gave off an aura of being empty.

What the hell?

Dalton walked to the front door and knocked. As a werewolf, he had great hearing. He listened for footsteps or for Cole working in the kitchen, but the house was quiet.

He could smell Cole's scent though, and it was recent. The scent trail headed off across the yard toward the trees. There was no way he was leaving without talking to Cole, so he stripped down to nothing in the cold air and shifted into his gray and white wolf.

The instant he shifted, his wolf surged to the front of his mind. The feelings he had for his mates intensified even more. He was full of energy, full of purpose. His fur kept him nice and warm. The urge to run coiled inside him like a spring. The need to find his mates drove out nearly every other thought.

Cole's scent called to him. Dalton could easily follow it out into the forest to find the other wolf. Before he started off, he lifted his muzzle and let out a long, joyful howl. It was good to be in wolf form again. It had been too many months and far too long since he'd shifted. Too many hotels and too many jaunts around the country on private planes had left him feeling disconnected from his wolf side. Cole knew that. That was why Cole chose to live out here in the mountains. Right now, he couldn't blame the man.

He set off at a run, following Cole's scent trail into the trees. The run through the forest and along the mountain slopes was a thrill, and he loved every moment of it. He was almost disappointed when he finally tracked Cole down.

Cole was repairing the fence around his property. He was setting one of the wooden rails back against the post that had been knocked askew at some point by a falling branch. Cole was wearing a cowboy hat, work boots, and a heavy work coat. Carhartt or something similar. He looked good, like he perfectly fit in the rustic scene.

As Dalton's wolf trotted out of the trees, Cole stood and turned to look at him.

A slow smile crossed Cole's face. Even though he'd never seen Dalton in wolf form, he clearly recognized Dalton's scent. "I heard your howl and figured you'd find me out here. Good to see you again, Dalton. You make a mighty fine wolf." He pulled off his work gloves and set them on the fence post. "But don't let that compliment go to your head like I know you will."

Dalton shifted back into human form so he could talk. The winter air was cold for walking around in naked skin, even for a werewolf. But he wasn't here for a winter sunbathing session. He intended to get Cole back to the house so they could have a man-to-man discussion over a beer and sort things out once and for all.

Cole let his gaze travel down Dalton's body, the smile lingering on his lips. "Gotta say I love the nudity. Now I feel overdressed."

Dalton snorted. He'd missed Cole and his quips. It had only been a few days, but already he'd been missing both his mates deeply.

"We need to talk," he said, cutting right to the chase.

Cole nodded. "I was wondering when you'd be by." He rubbed the back of his neck. "I went out to your place a couple of days ago to see you. No one was home." He shrugged. "I didn't have your number."

He cursed the loss of his phone. He had a new one now, but losing that phone during the blizzard had really caused him no end of problems and complications.

"I was in New York. I had a meeting of the board for one of my businesses and couldn't miss it." He was happy that Cole had come looking for him though. That was a good sign. "Maybe we can head back to the house and have a beer. Talk things out."

"Sounds good. Besides, it's going to be distracting as hell for me to carry on any kind of coherent conversation with you standing there buck naked." He jerked his chin toward the trees. "Fancy a race back to the house?"

Dalton grinned. "You're on."

He shifted back to his wolf. Cole shrugged out of his jacket, then stripped off the rest of his clothes and set his cowboy hat on the post over his gloves. Then he shifted. His wolf was about the same size as Dalton's, but with gray and brown fur and golden eyes.

Cole's wolf trotted over and nuzzled him. Dalton bit playfully at his ear. Then the two of them set off at a run back toward the cabin.

His heart soared as he sprinted through the trees with Cole right at his side. They tore along the trails, paws digging into the soft earth for traction. They wove through trees, crashed through underbrush, and scrambled up and down slopes, leaping a small stream on the way. Sometimes Dalton was in the lead, sometimes Cole surged ahead, but the race was always close. Until Cole pulled out ahead in the last stretch and won the race.

Back at the house, they both shifted back into human form. He gathered up his clothes and followed a naked Cole inside. He did get a great view of Cole's tight ass. Always a memorable sight. He loved the way Cole's muscles flexed as he walked. That view would never get old.

He dressed in the living room while Cole grabbed some new clothes from the bedroom and put them on.

"Beers in the fridge," Cole called to him from the bedroom. "Help yourself."

Dalton did exactly that, getting a beer for Cole as well.

Cole came back out in a shirt and jeans and immediately started up a fire in the fireplace. Soon the blaze was crackling merrily away.

Cole took a seat across from him and clinked his beer against Dalton's. "To the winner of our race."

Dalton couldn't help but laugh. "To the winner."

They both took a long drink.

"I let you win," Dalton said, still grinning. "You do realize that, right?"

"You keep telling yourself that," Cole replied cheerfully.

Dalton took another swig of his beer and sighed. Might as well jump right into this. He didn't think Cole would appreciate a lot of small talk.

"We need to talk about Cindy."

Cole leaned forward, staring down at his hands. "I went to see her too."

"What did she say?"

"I didn't talk to her. I sat there in my truck, staring at that business." He shook his head. "I even saw her drive off in her limo to go get a client."

"So you haven't talked to her since we dropped her off?" He found himself disappointed by the fact. He'd hoped Cindy had at least said something to Cole that might indicate they had a chance of saving things, of making this work.

"Not since then," Cole answered. He sighed. "It's amazing what a woman can do to a man. A few days ago I was living out here, minding my own business. And after meeting Cindy, I'm now watching her from my truck like some kind of creepy stalker. I don't know. Maybe it's a sign."

"What kind of sign?" He didn't like the sound of that. Not at all.

"A sign that this isn't going to work."

"What are you talking about? We're mates, damn it."

"Don't you think I know that? But she's a human.

She doesn't even believe in that kind of stuff."

"That night she did. When we told her. That night when she was with us, she believed it all. How could you forget that?"

Cole's expression darkened. "I never forget that. I can't. How could I forget one of the most perfect nights of my life?"

Dalton was getting angry himself. "So why the hell would you let something so perfect get away?"

"Maybe she realizes what we won't let ourselves see. Look, how many houses do you even own?"

"What the hell does that have to do with anything?"

"Just answer the question."

"I have a place in Boulder. A condo in New York. A beach house in St. Thomas. Another place in Seattle." He sounded defensive. That irritated him. He had nothing to feel defensive about. He'd made his money fair and square. He bought some house. Simple as that.

Cole barked out a laugh and shook his head. "See? That's crazy. What man needs four places to live, one of those in the Caribbean?" He paused. "Now that I think about it, it seems clear why you'd want a place in the Caribbean to get away from the snow. But still, it shows what I'm talking about. We're all too different from each other."

"That's what makes this perfect."

Cole looked at him as if he was crazy.

He pushed on. "I mean it. We're all different. We all bring something unique to the relationship. That makes what we have stronger."

"That's one way to look at it. Here's another one. I don't have any intentions of living in New York. My place is here. This is where I can be a wolf whenever I want. That race we ran together a minute ago? We can't do that in New York."

"There's always Central Park."

Cole laughed and punched him on the shoulder, then clinked his beer against Dalton's again. "Gotta hand it to you. You think quick on your feet." He took a drink. "But it doesn't change my point. One of the main reasons I live out here is because I can be a wolf whenever I want. No one freaks out. I'm not fined for public nudity. I can indulge my wolf's hunting instincts. I'm at peace out here."

Dalton leaned toward him. "Never once have I asked you to give this place up. So I don't know why it's an issue."

"Will Cindy want to live out here and drive in to work each day? What about you? Are you going to give up three houses and just live in Colorado?"

"You're making this harder than it has to be," Dalton growled. "It's like the two of you don't want this to work. It's almost as if you're afraid of it. Cindy and I can drive out here to see you easily enough. With me, it's not even an issue. I have private jets and helicopters." He leaned forward, pinning Cole with his stare. "She thinks it's over. That's what she told me when I went to see her. She even gave us the wrong phone number because she's so certain this can't work. She isn't even willing to try."

"Maybe she *is* willing to try," Cole said. "But maybe she's afraid because it's so crazy." His eyes were shining, his tone passionate. "What we shared was one of those fairy-tale moments in life. Like a perfect day." A smile flashed across his face. "Or it *ended* perfectly anyway. I don't know if starting with a blizzard and a car crash could ever be called perfect. But our wolves are too stupid to know that you can't have a perfect day like that *every* day. They think love is all you need. Maybe Cindy knows something we don't. Something we don't see because we're blinded by this whole 'mates' thing."

Hot anger and desperation shot through Dalton. "I refuse to believe that. You don't piss away something perfect just because it's hard or because you're afraid. We have the chance at something great. You don't turn your back on something like that. Not without a fight. How can we have a future if we don't believe we *can* have one?"

Cole leaned back and wiped a hand across his face. "I don't know what to say."

"How about you tell me how you feel? No bullshit. No games. I want to know you're in this with me. Because I intend to show Cindy exactly how I feel about her. I want you right by my side when I do."

"Hell, she gave you the wrong phone number." Cole ran a hand through his hair and laughed. "She almost treated us like a booty call." Cole stared out the window, his expression thoughtful. "Maybe she thought we were gonna ditch her, so she took the first shot. Look, she doesn't have a wolf inside insisting that we're her mates. So this is all different for her."

"I know."

Excitement flashed back into Cole's eyes. "If we love her, we have to prove it to her. Day in and day out. Until every part of her heart and mind believes it too."

Relief surged through him. That sounded like what he wanted to hear. Still, he wanted Cole on the record, because this would change everything for all three of them. "So where does that leave us?"

"It means we have to pull our thumbs out of our

asses and go find our mate."

Cole started to stand, but Dalton reached out and put a hand on his shoulder, stilling him. "I mean, where does that leave the two of us? I'm not giving up on you either. You might be a pain in my ass, and maybe you won that race. *Maybe*. But—"

"And I kicked your ass too. In that fight during the blizzard."

Dalton scowled. "Oh, the one where I came to the aid of a damsel in distress being chased by a crazy hermit werewolf?"

Cole tapped a finger against his lips. "She wasn't much of a damsel in distress. She hit me with a piece of firewood and ran into the storm."

"My *point* is, you're mine." Dalton leaned closer so he was staring right into the other man's eyes. "And I'm yours. And those are the simple facts."

"I'm not a follower," Cole warned. "I'm not joining your pack and becoming all beta to you. If that's what you expect, you might as well march right back out that door. If this has any chance of working, no one of us is more important than the other two. We have to find a balance." He shook his head slowly. "Which is probably why these relationships are so hard."

"We can do it. I know it. And you're right. If I start

pulling rank, I expect one of you to give me a swift kick in the ass."

"I'd be happy too."

Dalton ignored that. "I've had a lot of time to think, and you're right about one thing. I do need to get away from the city and out here to run in the wild. Running with you today...it meant a lot to me."

Cole met his gaze and held it. "It meant a lot to me too."

Dalton stood and held out his hand to the other wolf. "So are you with me? Do we make this love work? Do we go get our mate and make her see the light?"

Cole stood too, but he brushed aside Dalton's outstretched hand.

"Screw handshakes," he said gruffly. He pulled Dalton into an embrace, kissing him hard.

The kiss rocked him back on his heels. Inside, it was as if his head lit up and his heart glowed like a hot coal from the hearth. Love raced through him, in his blood, in his bones, and he knew how important Cole was to him—and always would be to him. This something they shared. Their wolf sides had easier access to the mystical side of love, and that warmed his heart even more.

Whatever challenges they faced, they would face

them together.

Finally, Cole ended the kiss. Dalton wanted more, of course, but he wanted Cindy here to enjoy it with them. He and Cole would have to prove their love to her, but again, he knew they were up to the challenge.

"So what's the plan?" Cole asked quietly.

"We call her friend at work. I think her name was Amanda. We find out when she's on break. And then we do something she will never forget. And if she forgets it, we do something else, day after day, until she gives in and lets us love her—"

"Or she takes out a restraining order," Cole finished, chuckling.

Dalton grinned. God, he loved this man. They were so different in some ways, but they fit together so perfectly. "Exactly, my friend."

"Man, I was already mourning losing her, but I'm damn glad you came out here and shook me out of my rut." He glanced out the window at the scenic view of trees and mountains. "It's easy to fall into a rut out here. You and Cindy shook me out of it the day of the blizzard. Guess I should've expected a little follow up might be necessary."

"Yeah, I didn't even tell you Plan B."

Cole's thick eyebrows rose in surprise. "Plan B?"

"The plan where I buy the land across the road from you and build a huge mansion. Then I walk out on porch naked every morning to get my newspaper. And I do it until you finally come begging to my door."

Cole laughed. "Hate to tell you this, but they don't deliver the paper out this far."

"I'm sure I can pay someone to do it. It would be worth it just so I could moon you every morning."

"You say that like it's a bad thing. I think the first thing I would invest in would be a pair of quality binoculars."

They both laughed, and Dalton slapped a hand down on Cole's shoulder. The other wolf had carved out a place in Dalton's heart so quickly it was almost enough to give him whiplash, but he wouldn't have it any other way.

Now they had one last job. Get to Cindy and prove to her that she belonged with them, and they belonged with her.

"Come on," he said. "Let's head into town. I want to talk to Cindy before she goes out tonight as a chauffeur."

Cole glanced at the clock on the mantel. "We don't have a lot of time."

"We do if we take the right vehicle." Dalton pulled

out his new cell phone. "I think this calls for a helicopter."

Cole's eyes went wide. "Damn. That's crazy."

"You know what makes a good impression?" Dalton stated. "Crazy."

Someone at the airport answered his call. He turned away from Cole for a moment so he could set this in motion. "Hi, my name's Dalton Kincaid. I need a helicopter right away. Cost is no object."

Some things were easy when you had a ton of money. Hiring helicopters was one of those things. What wasn't easy was winning the love of a woman like Cindy. But with Cole at his side, he knew they would do it.

She loved them. She simply hadn't opened her heart and let herself realize it yet.

CHAPTER ELEVEN

Cindy

It was one in the morning. Cindy was on her way back to Mirage after delivering her client back to his hotel for the night. The city streets only had sparse traffic. She loved to drive at night. It was so peaceful. You mostly got the green lights if you were on a main road. There wasn't a lot of traffic in your way. It was low stress, and right now, she really needed that.

She was tired and ready for the night to be over. At least her client, a tycoon visiting from New York, had been pleasant and had given a generous tip. So that took her mind off her problems for a little while. Working also helped. At least it was a distraction from a broken heart.

But now that she was alone again, all her pain and regrets flooded back in as if they'd never left.

There was no one to blame except herself and her own fear. She'd thought she was protecting herself from being hurt, but she'd only given herself a self-inflicted wound instead. All because she was afraid. Afraid of rejection, afraid of taking chances, afraid of something new. Maybe even afraid of being happy for the long term. That was why she was doing this safe job working as a chauffeur instead of throwing caution to the wind and trying to make it as an artist. She was afraid people wouldn't like her jewelry designs and that she would starve.

Fear was why she had rejected Dalton and Cole, driving them away every chance she had...

Amanda's voice came across the radio receiver, distracting Cindy from wallowing in self-pity. "Sweetie, this is HQ. Where you at?"

"I'm on my way back," Cindy replied. "Five minutes out, tops."

"Hurry back," Amanda said. "I mean, don't speed, but don't *not* speed, if you know what I mean."

Cindy had no idea what Amanda meant, but she was too tired to care much. She wanted to turn in the limo, finish her paperwork, and then clock out. After that, she faced a thrilling night on the couch. By herself. With microwave popcorn.

She reached up and drew out her necklace. She usually kept it hidden beneath her uniform, but right now, she wanted to touch it. Gently, she traced her thumb over the green stone. Touching it reminded her of Cole and Dalton. That hurt as much as it soothed, but she couldn't help it. At this moment, it was all she had.

A few minutes later, she pulled into the Mirage lot. She was one of the last drivers in for the night. The office lights were on, along with the garage lights. The place would be open until she and Amanda closed up shop. She glided the limo into her garage bay and parked. After logging her miles and route on her tablet computer, she got out and started for the door to the main office.

Long before she reached the door, Amanda burst through it. Her eyes were alight with excitement. Too much excitement for this time of night. Something was going on.

"Cindy! Drop everything and go outside to the parking lot!"

"What? The parking lot? I just drove through it. There are only two cars out there. Yours and mine."

Amanda took her arm and began to steer her toward one of the doors leading outside. "No, no. You gotta go outside, sweetie! Trust me, you're going to love this!"

Amanda pushed open the door and dragged her outside. They stood in the empty parking lot. The night sky was clear, and the stars looked brighter than ever. But it was also chilly out, with a cold wind blowing from the west.

Amanda stood next to Cindy with her arm around her shoulder. Her friend was staring up at the night sky.

"Um, so…" Cindy said, looking around and not seeing anything interesting. "Did you spot a UFO or something? Because there's not a lot happening out here right now. And it's a bit cold. So maybe we can go back inside?"

"Hush, now," Amanda replied, still staring at the sky. "Just wait."

She waited, hugging herself to keep warm and wishing she was in front of a fireplace. Maybe she could start a fire in one of the Dumpsters to get warm. It would be more exciting than waiting for whatever Amanda expected to happen to actually happen.

A moment later, she heard the distant sound of a helicopter. Amanda began to bounce on her toes, grinning from ear to ear.

"Here it comes!"

Cindy didn't have time to ask any questions. She spotted the helicopter lights as it approached. The sound of the rotors was soon a roar as the helicopter moved over a wide, clear spot in the parking lot away from trees or obstacles. As they watched, the helicopter gently touched down on the pavement.

She didn't know what to think. Was this some wealthy, big-shot client flying in at the last minute, wanting to be driven somewhere? She didn't have the heart for something like that tonight, no matter how much the client might tip. She'd already put in a full shift. Now she was only looking forward to heading home.

The helicopter blades were spinning down, gradually slowing. It was some kind of sleek civilian helicopter, but she couldn't see the passengers.

Then the doors opened. Dalton and Cole climbed out.

She froze, not sure if she was dreaming or not. But no matter how crazy it seemed to see her two shifters climb out of a helicopter that had landed in the Mirage parking lot, in her heart, she knew it was no dream.

She didn't know what to say or do. She only stood

there, gaping at them.

Amanda gave her a hug, leaned in close, and said, "They called and told me they were on their way and begged me to not let you leave before they arrived. What can I say? I'm a sucker for dashing men. Dashing men with helicopters. Don't worry, I'll fill out the rest of your paperwork for you. Go over and say hi to your friends."

With that, Amanda headed back inside.

Cindy only spared her the briefest glance. Her attention was focused on Cole and Dalton as they walked to her. Dalton was wearing a suit and a stylish overcoat. Cole was wearing jeans, cowboy boots, and a heavy work jacket. He even had a cowboy hat on, which he was holding down to keep the helicopter blades from blowing it off his head.

Her two men stopped in front of her. She wanted to throw herself into their arms. She wanted to cover them with kisses. She wanted to cry and laugh, probably both at the same time. But she only stood there, hugging herself and waiting.

"I've missed you something awful," Cole said, tipping his hat back and smiling at her warmly. His eyes were serious, intent on hers. "It's good to see you, Cindy."

"It's...it's good to see you too," she answered. It

was good to see them. Her heart felt like it was doing some kind of rumba of happiness inside her chest. They had flown out here...for her. Why would they do something that crazy? Unless the things they'd told her had all been true all along.

Dalton shoved his hands in the pockets of his overcoat, rocking on his heels as he stared at her. "I'm a stubborn man, Cindy."

"Is...is that right?" She didn't know what else to say. Those words hadn't been what she'd expected to hear.

He nodded. "Cole's a stubborn man too. Maybe it's something about being a werewolf. I don't know. But when we bring someone into our lives, we make it for keeps."

Cole broke in. "You crashed right into our lives." He put a hand on Dalton's shoulder, giving him a squeeze, even though his gaze remained locked on Cindy. "You changed us both. You brought us together. We need you. Simple as that."

She shook her head, all her doubts resurfacing. "You don't need me. You're both incredible people. You're both amazing. I can't—"

"Enough," Dalton said. He didn't say it cruelly, but there was command in his voice. And she obeyed, snapping her jaw shut on the last of her protests. She blinked at him, a little stunned.

He went on. "Right now, I want nothing else in the world more than I want to pull you into my arms and kiss you. It's taking every bit of self-control I have to stand here and talk about my feelings. I'd much rather show you. I'd rather show you over and over again until you believe me. Because actions speak louder than words." A slow, hot grin appeared on his face. A wicked grin. "If I touch you, I know I'm not going to be able to stop myself from kissing you. Then all these words will be out the window, and I rented that helicopter so the two of us could change your mind by pouring our hearts out."

"You belong with us," Cole said. "We belong with you. The three of us. Together. It's perfect." He shrugged, and his eyes twinkled as he grinned. "I've never been one for a lot of fancy talk. But I promise you, I'll make you happy. I'll walk beside you wherever you want to go. Hell, I'll even carry you there, if you'll allow it. But I want to be there. With Dalton, with you."

She opened her mouth to reply. To tell them yes, yes! A thousand times *yes*! That was what she wanted. She'd been a fool to push it away. She'd been weak and afraid, and she'd sabotaged herself. She wanted to thank them from the bottom of her heart for ignoring her protests and her tricks, for giving them the wrong number. She wanted to thank them for coming out here together to show her how much they cared.

But before she could get any of that past her lips, Dalton jumped in as if afraid she might turn them away before they'd said what they'd needed to say.

"I know it's a lot to ask. I know parts of it won't be easy. But it *is* love. These days away from you have only made me more certain of that than ever. I love you, Cindy." He looked at Cole. "Just like I love Cole. People might say we're moving too fast, that we should take it slow. But that isn't how I live my life. When my heart knows something, it knows it deeply, completely. I fought against my love for Cole, but I finally gave in. Don't make the same mistake I did and fight against our love."

Now Cole jumped in too. "Because we aren't going to give up on you. Not unless you really and truly feel nothing for either of us. But if you *do* feel something for us, I know you're brave enough to follow your heart, no matter where it might lead."

She blinked back tears, gritting her teeth and trying to hold in her emotions, to stop them from bursting out everywhere like water spraying from a broken pipe. The deep happiness and joy inside her warred with her regret at what she'd done, the risk she'd taken trying to drive them away. What was wrong with her? Why couldn't she simply take a chance on love and let herself be happy?

But she knew the reason. And it was time she told them.

"You're right," she said, her voice barely above a whisper. Her words trembled. It was a wonder they could hear her at all. "Thank you. I don't want you to give up on me. On us. I…I was afraid. I don't have any other excuse. I was afraid you would break my heart. I was afraid to believe that I could be happy. That I…could be loved."

She thought Dalton would be the first one to reach her, but Cole took the initiative, pushing back his cowboy hat and sweeping her into his arms. He kissed her. He kissed her deeply. He kissed her soundly. And when he finished, she had no doubts about how much he loved her. It was in the passion and the tenderness of his kiss. It was in the way he held her. It was in his eyes as he looked at her.

"Let those fears go," Cole said. "They're only fears, and they don't mean anything anymore. You have us. For as long as you want us. I love you, Cindy. I never want you to forget that."

Dalton came over, and she slipped from Cole's arms into Dalton's embrace effortlessly. Dalton's kiss was just as passionate, filled with just as much love and care as Cole's. It was rougher, overwhelming, yet filled with the care and kindness that underpinned everything Dalton did.

She was breathless, her mind spinning after two such kisses. She wanted to laugh and cry and do a happy dance on the roof of the limo. But right now she was content to simply stay here between them, in their arms, as they stood close to her.

Dalton tipped her chin upward so that she was looking him in the eyes. "Cole's right. Let those fears go, the same way I let my jealousy of Cole go and simply accepted that he loves you just as much as I do. Don't let anything drive the three of us apart. Every day from here on, every hour, we're going to be deepening the connection between us. Our love is only going to grow." He smiled, and it was one of the most genuine, most beautiful smiles she'd ever seen. "That's the wonderful thing about love. You can never have too much. So…will you be our mate, Cindy Taylor?"

Cole took her hand in his rough ones. "Yes. Will you be our mate?"

She closed her eyes and tilted her head back, feeling the chilly breeze on her skin and not caring. The air was fresh and clean. She felt like it was blowing away the dark clouds of fear and regret that had plagued her. She had a chance to make things right. She hadn't driven them away. She hadn't driven them away because they loved her.

And she loved them. God, how she loved them.

She opened her eyes again, and they were still waiting on her answer. She didn't know if this was a formal thing with werewolves, but she knew the words she needed to say. They came straight from the heart.

"Yes," she said. "I'd love to be your mate. Both of you. For as long as you'll have me."

Cole's eyes lit up with joy. "Then that means forever, girl, because I can't imagine a future without the two of you."

"That goes double for me," Dalton said, a fierce love and pride shining in his eyes as he looked at each of them. He put one arm around her and the other around Cole. "We belong together. I didn't think I believed in it, but fate stepped in to make it happen."

Cindy laughed, pulled out her necklace, and held it up so they could see. "And luck. This stone's supposed to make you lucky in love."

Cole smirked. "Guess it doesn't make you lucky to avoid accidents during a blizzard though."

"If she hadn't crashed, we wouldn't be here right now," Dalton chided. He winked at her. "So that's the best good luck charm I've ever seen. You should sell those. You'd make a fortune."

She laughed, feeling the final remaining bits of tension and bleakness of the last week fade away. "You're my favorite billionaire in the world, Mr. Dalton Kincaid." She kissed him just to underline the point.

"Hey," Cole protested. "What about those of us who aren't able to rent a helicopter at the drop of a hat?"

"You're right," she said, giving him a kiss too. "You're my favorite mountain man in the world, Mr. Cole Marsten."

Cole raised an eyebrow. "Technically, I'm not a mountain man."

"You live in the mountains. And you're a man. I know, because I've seen you naked."

"Can't argue with that logic," Cole drawled, stealing another kiss. "Damn, we're lucky to have you in our lives, pretty lady."

"Not as lucky as I am," she said, and meant every word.

Dalton glanced across the parking lot. "Speaking

of helicopters. I happen to have one on hand. Are you interested in a little nighttime helicopter ride around Colorado? We can swing out to Denver and ooh and ahh over the city lights."

She grinned. "That sounds wonderful. And then what?"

Cole looked at Dalton too, waggling his eyebrows. "Yeah, Mr. Billionaire. And then what?"

"Well," Dalton said, doing his best to mimic Cole's easy drawl. "I say we head back to my place and fuck each other's brains out."

She giggled. "So romantic!"

Dalton kissed her. "What do you say, my beautiful little mate? Make this a perfect night for us."

"I'd love to," she whispered, her heart overflowing with happiness. The three of them headed for the helicopter, arm in arm, and she never looked back.

EPILOGUE

Cindy

Las Vegas, Nevada
Seven months later…

"So should I stand or hit?" Cindy asked, staring at her cards and then eyeing the blackjack dealer's cards. "I don't want to bust."

Cole leaned over from his place at the blackjack table next to her to peer at her cards. "Cindy, my love. You have a four of spades and a two of hearts. That adds up to six."

She squinted at the dealer, trying to read him. But the dealer had a perfect poker face. In fact, he seemed a little like a robot. "So…I call?"

"You don't 'call' in blackjack," Dalton informed her. "That's poker."

Dalton was glowering at his cards. Her favorite billionaire had been losing ever since he'd taken a seat at the dealer's table. Even though this was Cindy's first time playing and she barely had an idea what she was doing, she'd already won more money than Dalton had. Or maybe that was the wrong way to say it. So far, she'd *lost* less money than Dalton had.

She tried not to feel smug about that…and failed.

She'd make it up to her grumbly wolf later. In their big suite on the top floor of the Bellagio, on the huge bed with the incredible view of Vegas, she'd make Dalton forget every single dollar he'd lost tonight.

She knew Cole would be right there with her, giving a helping hand, and helping…other parts.

Cole leaned in and kissed her on her bare shoulder. Since she was wearing a strapless evening gown, that was easy enough. It was a tender kiss, full of affection. She knew he'd be saving his passionate kisses for when he and Dalton could get her alone. Get her out of this dress. And get their hands, and their lips, all over her.

She had to suppress a shudder of pure delight.

Honestly, who cared about a card game like twenty-one when there was sex on the table? And the bed. And the shower...

God, her horniness had reached a whole new level since arriving in Vegas.

"You have to focus," Cole told her softly, his voice amused. But when she met his eyes, she could see the hot desire burning there. Her two werewolves were experts at telling when she was turned-on. "Otherwise you're going to lose as badly as Dalton is."

"I heard that," Dalton growled.

Cole told her to hit, so she politely asked for another card. It was a queen of hearts. She was at sixteen. She decided to live dangerously and hit again. The card was a five of diamonds.

She looked at Cole, who let out a whoop that had half the casino looking their way.

"So I won, right?" she asked.

"Well, only if the dealer doesn't get to twenty-one."

After Dalton busted, the dealer also busted.

Cole gave her a tight hug and kissed the top of her head. "I knew you were lucky from the first moment I saw you."

"It's my necklace," Cindy said with a laugh. She touched the silver and malachite necklace she'd made. The same one she'd been wearing the night of the blizzard.

Cole glanced over at Dalton. "Maybe she can make you one of those. You're the unluckiest gambler I've ever met."

"Eh," Dalton said. "I lost on purpose."

They both looked at him deadpan.

Dalton's face filled with mock outrage. "What? Can't a wolf let his mates win once in a while? It's not fair me being so handsome and ripped and debonair and then also win all the time too."

"You forgot 'crazy rich' in your list," Cindy said with a wry smile.

Dalton's expression grew serious. "I wasn't rich until I met both of you."

Her heart melted. Her eyes teared up a little.

Cole leaned against the blackjack table, eyeing Dalton. "That's pretty cheesy."

Dalton's face broke into a wide grin. "You loved it though."

"I always do."

"And so do I," Cindy added quickly, feeling a

wonderful warmth spreading through her body. She had never believed she could be this happy. She hadn't thought it was even possible. Every day seemed better than the last. Their lives were so filled with love that it left her feeling complete, cherished, and happy.

"I think it's time to end on Cindy's win," Cole said, his words thick with desire. She could tell what he was thinking about. She might not be a shifter, but she could read her mates very well. "And we can head back to the suite."

"A perfect idea." Dalton caught her hand, lifted it to his lips, and gently kissed her knuckles. "What do you think, Ms. Taylor? Shall we retire for the evening?"

She was grinning even as she felt her cheeks heat. "Oh, I don't want to *retire*."

Dalton's gaze intensified. "Then let me put it another way. Shall we head upstairs and break the bed? Maybe test if the walls in our fancy suite really are soundproof?"

"That is a wonderful idea, Mr. Kincaid."

"You're right. It is a great idea," Cole added. "Good thing he's a better lover than a gambler."

The dealer still wore a carefully neutral expression. She knew he'd overheard them, and she was a bit embarrassed about that. One thing she still hadn't gotten used to was how open and direct werewolves could be about things like sex. They saw it as a natural part of life, not anything shameful. She liked that.

Dalton gave the dealer a huge tip as they left the table. She approved of that too. The dealer had been a good sport. Especially when dealing with a player like her, one who'd never played blackjack before in her life.

Cindy walked between Dalton and Cole, a big, handsome man on each side of her. She loved it. Cole had his arm around her shoulders. Dalton had his arm around her waist. They got a few looks from some of the other patrons, but she was used to that by now. It didn't bother her. She didn't let other people's opinions drag her happiness down.

And she was happy. Deliriously happy. She was in it's-scary-how-happy-I-am-right-now territory. But the thing was, she wasn't scared. These two incredible men were there for her, and they were there for each other. They might be opposites in many ways, coming from wildly different backgrounds, but those differences only seemed to make their love stronger.

It was love, too. And it had always been love. Since that first night all the way to today, here in Vegas, it had been love. Sure, that love had only deepened with time, but the passion burned as brightly as it always had.

Wrecking her limo in a blizzard had turned out to be the best thing that had ever happened to her.

Speaking of her old job, she'd left Mirage two months ago. Her coworkers had thrown her a huge party, wishing her well. Amanda had been in tears, but Cindy made sure they still got together for girl's nights.

Why had she left Mirage? Well, because she was going into business for herself. Some people might judge her for not doing it all on her own, but she was only doing the best she could.

It was a huge, terrifying step. Dalton had practically begged her to accept him as a "patron." He'd had a workshop built for her at his newly constructed mansion across the road from Cole's cabin. Cole had helped with all the shop set up, delivering equipment and building cabinets and tables. When Dalton had told Cole that he didn't have to build everything by hand, Cole had only looked at him and said, "Yes, I do." After that Dalton had dropped it. Her two mates had reached an understanding, as they almost always did.

But Dalton had also helped her reach out to artisan and gift shops as places to sell her jewelry. He'd even hired a web developer to make her a website, all so she could focus on making jewelry.

She loved it. She was good at it, not great. She

didn't have an inflated opinion of her current skill. She was good, but she had improvements to make, things still to master. But she was one hundred percent eager to make those improvements and master all she could. She wanted people to love her jewelry. She wanted her customers to feel beautiful. To feel happy. She felt happy making them happy.

Even though she wasn't making nearly enough to live on yet—she was kind of sponging off of Dalton right now, living with him and Cole in a freaking *mansion*— she was still full of determination to pull her own weight and make her business a success. She was inspired, and she knew Dalton and Cole loved that inspiration and the excitement she showed.

The three of them had moved into Dalton's mansion, which was almost complete. They were still dealing with construction and contractors and work crews, but she was used to it by now, and she certainly wasn't complaining. In her humble opinion, no one having a mansion built around them had any right to complain, ever.

Surprisingly, they still went to Cole's place at least once a week, just to sit by the fire together. Dalton's mansion had four big, fancy fireplaces, but there was something about that fireplace at Cole's house that warmed all three of their hearts…

They headed through the casino, and she was amazed—and a little intimidated—by how fancy and beautiful the hotel was. All the colors seemed so rich and deep. Purples, golds, marble. There were incredible glass flowers along the lobby ceiling, bursting with vivid colors. Botanical gardens with lush tropical flowers—real ones this time. The place even had a fine art gallery, not to mention the fountain show that never seemed to get old. Oh, and chocolate fountains that sent streams of chocolate pouring down from the ceiling, the streams sealed away by glass. The whole thing was simply astounding to a small-town girl from Texas.

They reached the elevator leading to the penthouse suites. They had a special card that allowed access to the top floor luxury suites. It all felt so exclusive and decadent. She still wasn't used to living this way.

Honestly, she didn't think she ever would be. Maybe that was for the best. She didn't need to end up a spoiled princess who'd forgotten where she came from. Maybe she didn't fit in with high-society types, but her two men never treated her wrong, never made her feel like less of a person. And that was all that mattered: how much they loved her.

Inside the elevator, Dalton drew her close and

kissed her. It was a tender, loving kiss. One she could sense was hinting at coming passion. He drew back, looking into her eyes with a charming smile on his face.

"Thank you for coming here with us, Cindy," he said, his mellow baritone setting her heart to beating faster.

Cole moved up behind her, pressing his body against hers. She bit her lip as her core tightened with desire. She could feel how hard he was, his erection pressing against her ass. He pushed aside her hair and kissed his way up her bare neck, sending shivers through her body.

"He's right," Cole murmured against her hot skin. "And we're going to show you exactly how thankful we are. Over and over again."

She moaned, closing her eyes and tilting her head to give him better access to her neck. God, she loved these two men so much. How had she ended up so lucky?

She finally caught her breath enough to sigh out a reply. "You don't have to thank me for coming to Las Vegas and being treated like a queen, you two silly wolves."

The elevator door opened. They headed down the wide hallway with stunning light fixtures and high-end art, all very classy and beautifully designed. Inside their suite, things were even fancier. Huge windows with gorgeous views, a wet bar, orchids, furniture she was a little hesitant to sit on because it looked so expensive. Champagne sat in an ice bucket along with three champagne flutes. She wandered over to the big windows, drawn by the expansive view.

Outside the sky glittered with stars, and below that, the ground glittered with city lights for what seemed like thousands of miles. This room had a view of the fountain and the strip, with the Eiffel Tower from the Paris casino all lit up across the street. She wanted to open the big window and tell everyone far below on the streets of Vegas to never give up hope. To keep chasing their dreams. That love was out there somewhere for them. She wanted to reassure them that sometimes you had to travel a long road—and sometimes even crash off that road—to find happiness, but that happiness could be found.

It was out there, just waiting.

Her two men came over to join her at the window. She hugged Cole and then Dalton, emotions caught in her throat so that she could barely speak.

"I love you both so much." She blinked back happy tears. "Finding you has been the most wonderful thing in my life. It's like a wonderful dream where I never wake up."

Cole was watching her with love in his eyes. "Same for us, beautiful. You complete us." He grinned and shook his head. "Hell, without you, there'd be no us. I love you, Cindy." He glanced at Dalton. "And I love you too, you rich, city-slicker bastard."

Dalton's grin and the warmth in his eyes told her that he knew that was Cole being Cole and it didn't ruffle his fur. Cole loved to give Dalton a hard time, but it was clear from every action Cole took that he would die for Dalton, that he loved him deeply, that they were good, true friends. That lifted her heart even more.

Dalton kissed Cole, then kissed her. "I love you both. Every day, every hour, that love just deepens. You've both made me one happy wolf. And I'm going to spend the rest of my life showing you exactly how much I appreciate that."

Her heart melted, hearing that. Now her vision was even blurrier with more happy tears, and her throat tight with emotion.

Without another word, the three of them went inside the suite's huge master bedroom. And then their little private party *really* started.

~ About the Author ~

Zoey Thames writes romance of all flavors, but right now she's obsessed with billionaires and sometimes hot werewolves! She watches superhero movies and loves peppermint coffee.

Her book *Curves for Three*, the first of the Quick & Sexy Wolves series, released in May 2016 and *Curves for Fighters* released in September 2016. *Curves for Shifters* released in October 2016. *Curves for Wolves* is the newest in the series. *Table for Three* is the first book in her new Big Girls and Billionaires series of contemporary MMF ménage. *A Fashionable Threesome* is book two, *Room for Three* is the third installment, *Maid for Three*'s number four, and *Three for the Sea* is the most recent addition to the series.

She's busy at work writing the next book in the series, filled with billionaires and the curvy women who love and are loved by them.

You can find Zoey Thames here

Website: http://www.ZoeyThames.wordpress.com

~ Also by Zoey Thames ~

Curves for Fighters
Quick & Sexy Wolves Book Two
Zoey Thames

Two powerful werewolves. One irresistible woman.
Ruth, a curvy, good-hearted Oklahoma girl, drives limos for Mirage Confidential, a company that specializes in chauffeuring wealthy paranormals around New York City. When she's dispatched to a rundown martial arts studio to pick up a billionaire werewolf alpha, she's certain she has the wrong information. What would a rich and powerful man like Brian Barrington be doing at a fighting ring in the Bronx? Yet, after watching an

intense sparring round between the attractive Brian and his equally hot MMA trainer, the sight of the two half-naked men has her imagination in erotic overdrive. And that was before she accidentally stumbles upon both men locked in passion in the back of the gym. She's going to need a miracle to survive this pair of clients, who already have her internal thermostat dangerously close to overheating...

Brian might be one of the world's richest and most powerful wcrewolves, but that doesn't mean he's let it go to his head. In his downtime, he trains as a mixed martial artist with his best friend and fellow shifter, Dominic. Being bisexual, they enjoy each other's company in every way possible, but what they really enjoy is sharing a woman between them. And the sweet little BBW in the chauffeur uniform is already setting them both on fire. Trouble is, winning the trust of the fascinating human woman is trickier than either of them imagined. Both men agree, she's one worth fighting for, but are they ready for a no-nonsense, full-bodied country girl with curves that have them ready to beg for mercy?

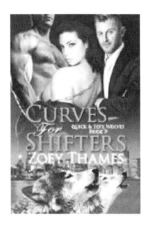

Curves for Shifters
Quick & Sexy Wolves Book Three
Zoey Thames

With these two alphas, a curvy girl will need all the luck she can get.

Michelle Ross always brings her lucky charm bracelet along for the ride when she's chauffeuring shifter clients for Mirage Confidential. So when a bodyguard refuses to let her onto the luxury jet where she's supposed meet her client, the billionaire werewolf Aaron Duval, she's forced to get creative. And ends up barging in on one of the sexiest things she's ever seen. Aaron Duval and Jackson Smith, two drop-dead gorgeous males, are locked in a passionate kiss no one else was supposed to witness. Now there's going to be consequences. Too bad this time she left her lucky bracelet behind in the limousine...

Alpha Aaron Duval can't believe things have gone this wrong. Even though he runs a successful security firm providing bodyguards for the rich and powerful, one beautiful human woman has just evaded his guards and crashed his kiss. A kiss with his business rival and ex-lover, Jackson Smith, a man Aaron's wolf still considers his mate. Now Jackson is claiming the human is a spy, that Aaron is plotting something underhanded, and he's demanding a hearing before the High Shifter Council. In Chicago. Tonight. Oh, and the curvy chauffeur? Jackson's practically kidnapped her to stop her from talking to the media about their kiss. One thing is certain—this is no way to impress a woman his wolf is also claiming as a mate.

Jackson knows right away the hot little BBW is two things: his mate and big trouble. Even if she's not a reporter, he can't risk her selling the story of him kissing his business rival to a gossip rag right before he expands his security company. Unfortunately, that leaves him in conflict with his inner wolf. The stubborn beast believes both his ex-lover Aaron and Michelle are his mates. But Jackson's not above pulling out every trick in the book to win. He has that alpha pride after all. And if that means a fight in the ring with Aaron to prove himself right, well, he hasn't trained half his life as a mixed martial artist for nothing. Too bad he still secretly loves the man...

Curves for the Cage
Quick & Sexy Wolves Book Four
Zoey Thames

A billionaire werewolf. A champion cage-fighter. A curvy human girl who will bring them to their knees...

Dixie Campbell always wears a smile for the wealthy paranormal shifters she chauffeurs around Las Vegas. But when billionaire alpha Pierre Bouchard and his fighter, Mackey Mackay, arrive for a high-profile shifter MMA tournament, things quickly get off on the wrong foot. Pierre might be handsome as sin, but everything Dixie does seems to irritate him. She much prefers Mackey, the tough-on-the-outside, sweet-on-the-inside, built-for-sex cage fighter. But when the two scorching-hot men share a kiss in front of her, she thinks her fantasies of Mackey are over. Until she learns they're both bisexual. And they like threesomes... Too bad the hot, alpha Pierre seems to hate her guts.

Pierre is in Las Vegas for one reason: to see his lover Mackey win the tournament. Among all the highly ranked wolves, jaguars, and bears, Mackey's favored to win. But Pierre doesn't expect Mackey to start seeing their curvy human chauffeur as his second mate. Even though Pierre and Mackey are bi, they haven't shared a woman in a ménage in over a year. After all, Mackey is his true mate, not some sexy BBW whose incredible curves happen to ignite both their fleeting desires. Even if Pierre can't stop wanting her either.

While Mackey is battling in the cage, Pierre fights to keep Dixie at arm's length. Mackey doesn't need the distraction, and neither does he. An unscrupulous billionaire jaguar shifter has just made a million-dollar bet against Mackey, and the shady jaguars lurking in the shadows make it clear they'll do anything to win. And now, just as things are heating up in the cage, they've set their sights on Dixie…

Table for Three
Big Girls and Billionaires
Zoey Thames

Set the table for a scorching threesome...

Josie Smith, a hardworking waitress at the Highland Grill, doesn't believe her friend's prediction that Josie's life is about to change. So what if her horoscope says she's about to meet one, maybe two, mysterious strangers? They'd probably just be bill collectors. Mysterious men she could do without. The last guy she dated was mysterious, all right—he was a pathological liar. And the one before that did nothing but take jabs at her plus-size, curvy figure. But when her friend points out Lucas and Dan, the two hotties who've become regulars at the Highland Grill, Josie can only laugh. Sure, they're sexy as sin with their black leather jackets and big, shiny motorcycles. But sadly, she isn't exactly their type. She'd caught them in a scorching-hot embrace in the parking lot one night, and even Josie isn't foolish enough to pine away over two gay guys.

Lucas Pearce has more money than he can spend in several lifetimes. He's a powerful, respected, old-money billionaire, and has a man he loves and trusts—tech mogul Dan Jackson. Both of them are bisexual, and both agree their hearts are big enough for one more. When they discover the Highland Grill, they immediately fall for the beautiful, Rubenesque Josie Smith. Josie believes they're just city boys who ride in every Friday on their motorcycles for the great food. But the boys are hungry for more than just the Friday night special. They want the curvy waitress with the kind smile and the warm eyes— and they intend to do whatever it takes to get her. So when things go south at the Highland Grill, Lucas and Dan think they've got it all under control. But it isn't long before they realize they might not be as all-powerful as they'd thought, and Josie might not be as easy to win as they'd imagined...

Printed in Great Britain
by Amazon

41425183R00139